PALMS TO THE GROUND

Contents

PALMS TO THE GROUND

Hush, Little Baby, Don't Say a Word

"What is it, Calman? What's the matter?" Bridgette Pulowitz twirled the Lucite rod that dangled from Calman's blinds. She squinted at the morning sunlight he tried each day to postpone. "You'll be late for school, love. Why haven't you washed?"

Calman's mother was statuesque. Her face was framed in thick, shoulder-length hair dyed jet black every six weeks. Her impeccably matched summer ensemble flattered her five-foot-ten-inch frame. She leaned over Calman's bed and pressed her hand to his forehead. He felt the cold metal of her bangles as they slid against his eyebrows. "Are you sick?"

Calman lay supine, arms out, hands flopped over the sides of his bed. Two pillows rested under his knees. His fan was circulating an itchy odor of hair spray. "My back hurts. I can't move." Calman felt fortunate to be in his own bedroom at a time of temporary paralysis. Lucky, too, that his back had weakened on the day of his last exam of the school year. He strained to see his mother's pained stare, then settled his eyes on his life-size James Bond 007 poster across the room. He wondered if Bond ever complained of an aching back, or if he ever complained at all. Maybe the movie directors just cut those scenes so 007 could save the world standing upright and away from his mother.

"*Ow*," Calman yelled at his mother's poking and pushing. The pain, which had kept him awake since dawn, forked in pulses up to his shoulder blades.

His mother shook her head and slid Calman's desk chair over to his bed to sit down. "Oh, Calman," she said apologetically, picking at her cuticles. "Your father and I have been so busy. Do you need some attention? Is that it?" Her cell phone rang from inside the pocket of her blazer. She flipped it open. "What? What is it? Seven? No, eight. I said eight! Not nine. Not seven. Eight. *Do it*. I'll be in the office soon—call me there." She clapped it closed.

Drifting in a sea of dark blue cotton sheets, Calman stared blankly at the ceiling.

"Haven't we told you," she continued, as if the phone interruption had had the duration and importance of a hiccup, "if you need attention, you should say, 'Mom, I need you to pay attention to me'? If you're straight with us, we can respond."

She paused, likely waiting for a dialogue. "Calman, I can't read your mind. I'm not with you all day. I don't know all the stresses in your life. If something's bothering you, then let's talk about it. Tell me, what is it?"

Up close, Calman could see just how precisely his mother outlined her lips before she colored them in. "My back," he said, plaintively. "It hurts."

A buzzing sound, like a party of horseflies, exploded into the hallway over a steamy, drenched rendition of "Love Me Tender."

"Crap. Your father does this every time he's in the shower. That snooze alarm drives me crazy." She hurried out with exasperated momentum. Calman watched her leave, saw her hit her funny bone on his bookcase that protruded into the doorway, heard her curse the day's beginning.

He took a deep breath and stared at his bookcase. It was top-heavy with hardcovers in alphabetical order by title. Size order, said his mother, would be too asymmetrical. No order, she stated, would waste time. Ever since he had developed a sufficient attention span, Calman's parents had taken turns reading to him at night. Mondays and Wednesdays were Calman's nights to choose a story. Tuesdays and Thursdays were saved for thick books on healing, hurting, controlling, feeling, fearing, connecting, channeling, growing, and inner peace. *Mother Goose* sat squeezed between *The Mind/Body Link* and *Ourselves, Our Egos*. And *Curious George* was hidden behind *Fifty Ways to*

Leave Your Mother. "Getting in touch, staying in touch. It took us years of therapy to get that far," his mother would say. "You don't know how lucky you are," his father would add.

Shortly after the noise stopped, Calman's mother returned to her seat next to Calman's bed. She sat on the edge of the chair and meditated for a few moments before she spoke again. Calman watched the familiar routine. She closed her eyes, rolled her head limply from side to side, and inhaled through her nose. She shrugged her shoulders, then exhaled and dropped them abruptly, swinging her arms and wiggling her hands at the floor.

"Why don't you join me, Calman? Let's shake some tension out through our fingertips and make room for positive energy."

Calman noticed how pleased she looked at having the opportunity to release tension and dry her nail polish simultaneously.

"Calman, you're not participating here," she said with a patronizing lilt.

"Sorry." Calman flapped his hands for her.

"Now, where were we?" she sighed.

The throbbing in Calman's lower back triggered a similar pounding behind his eyes as he saw her peek surreptitiously at her watch.

"Oh, yes. Something's bothering you. Is it school? Are you upset that you're almost done with the eighth grade?"

"No."

"Did you finish your homework on the computer last night while Daddy and I were at the concert?"

"Yes." His homework assignment had consisted of eighteen wordy math problems and a short paragraph for his own obituary. "Please note, children, that one would not want to be remembered for bad grammar," his English teacher had cautioned. Calman took a long time deciding his fate. He finally wrote: "Calman Pulowitz died today in Boston, Massachusetts. It was an accident. He tripped onto the trolley tracks after someone tied his shoelaces together. He broke his ankle, then cracked his head open on the pavement and was flattened by an approaching train. Witnesses say he didn't scream. He wasn't even surprised. He leaves behind a mother, a father, and a grandmother who lives in Cleveland. His parents told reporters that they are sad and feel guilty that they left him to wander around alone, without a chaperone. Calman Pulowitz will always be remembered for keeping his room clean . . . and for his good grammar." The spell-check on his computer said Pulowitz should be pullouts. Calman Pullouts.

"Calman," said his mother with renewed energy, "maybe you are experiencing a . . . a sort of post-party depression. You know, now that your bar mitzvah is over. It's hard to believe that all that planning was for one day, isn't it? By the way, you never told me what Cousin Shirley gave you."

Calman remembered a mettlesome Cousin Shirley in the ninth row waving her cowboy hat above the congregation and yelling shortly after his Torah reading, "Atta boy . . . Mazel tov, kid." Related to the family through a failed marriage, Cousin Shirley was a retired oil executive turned migrant fruit-picker with a wheezy Brooklyn accent.

"A Swiss Army Knife," answered Calman. Cousin Shirley had told him it was the only thing in life he'd ever need.

"Never a dull moment with your father's side of the family."

Calman closed his eyes for a second. He heard his father shut off the shower water, then the screeching and accelerating of impatient commuters at the traffic light below his window.

"Well, what do you think, Calman?" asked Bridgette Pulowitz after a lengthy pause.

"About what?" asked Calman, thinking she meant his opinion of Cousin Shirley.

"Do you think you are upset that your bar mitzvah is over?" she repeated emphatically.

"No, not really."

Calman's mother leaned back in her chair and crossed her arms in her lap. "Calman, if it's not school, and it's not the bar mitzvah, what is it? Is there something else you want to talk about?"

"No." Calman knew she was running late. He felt fidgety, but his movements, any movement, hurt his back even more. His mother stood up to straighten the painting above Calman's head. It was a sailboat on a sea, painted by a friend of a friend of the family. At least once a week, she would tilt it with her thumb slightly to the right. And nearly every third or fourth night, before bedtime, Calman's father would tip it ever so slightly to the left. More than once the waves in that picture had come alive in Calman's nightmares and made him seasick.

"There's nothing on your mind?" asked his mother. "That's rather hard to believe, Calman."

He shifted slightly. The pressure tugged at him from behind and smothered him from above. Staying still, he decided, was the only answer to the pain.

Bridgette Pulowitz rubbed her temples in tiny circles. "You know, maybe the trip to Seattle—"

"It's not Seattle," Calman corrected. "Walla Walla's on the other side of Washington."

"Yes, well, in any event, maybe the trip out West to visit that pen pal of yours isn't such a good idea. Maybe your father and I should've thought of something else to give you for your bar mitzvah." She searched for a reaction from Calman. "I mean, I'm not so sure you can handle a trip right now. They've never met you before. They wouldn't have any idea how to interpret something like this. I know you want to go, lovebug, but you know how nervous I was about this trip from the start. I should never have let your father talk me into it. How would you feel if we canceled it altogether, Calman?"

"Okay," answered Calman, a little too quickly. "I guess," he said as a follow-up to soften any perceived eagerness. But he knew—and she knew—there was no turning back. His flight was booked, and their flight to Florida had been booked, too, for months.

mother shook her head and walked out, mumbling thing about an appointment. Calman lay very still and ned to her apprise his father of the situation. He heard nly fragments, when they didn't whisper. "One-word answers," he heard her say, and "Maybe you can talk to him." Then he heard his father: "All right, I'll make an appointment with his therapist."

A few moments later, Calman's father walked into Calman's bedroom with a glass of bottled water and a B-complex vitamin.

"I hear you're having a bit of trouble this morning," he said, as he kissed Calman's forehead gently.

It's my back, Calman thought, but didn't say.

Alone in his room, with his backache and bran muffin that his parents had left him, Calman thought about his upcoming trip to Washington State. It was just ten days away, which was really only one week after the last day of school, and that was barely enough time for emotional preparation. Just ten short go-by-before-you-know-it days until he would be carted off to the other side of the country because his therapist thought it was a good idea. For weeks he had overheard his mother's protests: *My baby . . . his first time away from home alone . . . these people we're sending him to could be ax murderers . . . my God, in this day and age . . . my only son, my reason for living.* "Bridgette," his father would say in his calm, exasperated voice. "You're being overprotective. You know the schools have thoroughly screened the family. I told you, I've talked with the father, he's a doctor and an upstanding citizen, the family is well established in the town. Besides, thousands of kids do this all the time through exchange programs. It's not like he's going to Siberia, for God's sake. Let the boy live a little."

What had he been doing up until now if not living? Calman wondered. Living was suddenly becoming a scary enterprise, for neither his mother nor his father knew what the *real* threat was: his pen pal. They'd never read his pen pal's letters, obviously typed on an old-fashioned typewriter, so they looked like ransom notes. They had never even asked to see them, claiming something about respecting his privacy. But if they had looked at any of them, just one, they, too, would have been alarmed by the disturbing doodles along the edges. Not to mention what the letters described.

No, his and his pen pal's worlds were as far apart as their postmarks, and Calman was sure they should remain so. At the very least, Calman preferred his perceptions about who he was and what his life was like to remain unchallenged. "To write is to reveal," his English teacher had once proclaimed. To write is to hide, Calman now knew.

Lying still and staring at a fly, Calman thought about the letters that had come once, sometimes twice a week for the last nine months, ever since he had signed up for Pen Pals of the United States. Some anti-techno baby boomer thought up the program, which was supposed to prompt a resurgence in hand-written letters. His parents just loved it, seeing that his father had perfect handwriting and his mother reminisced with nauseating frequency about her own pen pal and the letters she had sent when she was Calman's age, all adorned with smelly, glow-in-the-dark, beady-eyed hippie stickers from her vast collection.

He still had his pen pal's letters, every one, including copies of all the letters he had sent so he could remember what he had written. Quickly, so as not to endure more than a moment of throbbing pain, Calman reached below his bed and pulled up a stack of mail. He took out the first letters he and his pen pal had sent to each other at the beginning of the school year, and read them again.

Dear Rizzy,

Hi. How are you? My name is Calman Pulowitz, but you probably know that. This is the third letter I've ever sent to anyone. The first two were to my grandmother in Cleveland, but she never wrote back and anyway my mother told me that she has bad eyesight and has trouble reading my handwriting. I probably got that from her. Bad eyesight, I mean. I just got glasses and so far all they do is make me dizzy.

Anyway, that's why I'm typing this letter. I hope you can understand it.

I don't really know what to say. My parents said this

program would be good for me, to write to someone, but I don't really have anything interesting to write about.

I have light brown hair, and I'm sort of short, at least compared to almost everyone else in my class.

I'm an only child, but I wouldn't mind having one or two sisters around, or brothers, I guess. My father is a designer at a book publishing company. He does a lot of covers for novels and stuff. My mother is an interior decorator. She makes sure that things match and that they're in the right place in a house. Like furniture. She likes black and white. Almost everything big in our apartment is black or white, and most of it is uncomfortable. I don't know about all of it because I'm not really allowed in the living room. Do you have any brothers or sisters?

School's okay. I'm in the eighth grade, but you probably already know that, too. I like English, but I hate science. We're studying rocks now, and we're supposed to keep a pet rock in our desk. My father bought me a mouse pad that says "Rock On." I don't see why having a pet rock is such a big deal. It's just a rock. My mother says she likes the idea of a pet rock because she says you don't have to scoop its poop. That's a law here. Anyway, our apartment building doesn't allow pets. Do you have a pet?

Have you ever been to Boston? A lot of people come to visit here this time of year because our trees turn colors other than green. And I guess it is kind of pretty. I don't like winter much since my parents are usually in a bad mood because they

*have to drive in the snow. And I have to wear my boots to
school.*

*Well, I better go. My grandmother is coming to stay with us
today. She's supposed to be here soon. She got two hundred
dollars off on her airplane ticket because last time she came here
she volunteered to take a later flight. They had too many people
on the plane. She said it wasn't a mistake—the airlines always
sign up more people than they need because they figure that
some of them won't show up. She said she gave up her seat and
sat in the airport in Cleveland for an extra hour just so she
could see us another time. My grandmother gives up a lot for us.
I think my mother forgets this because my grandmother always
reminds her.*

*Well, I hope I didn't bore you. If you don't want to be pen
pals, I'll understand.*

Sincerely,

Calman Pulowitz

*P.S. I looked up Walla Walla on the map. It's 2,800 miles
from Boston. That's far. It takes me nine minutes to walk to
school, which is only one quarter of one mile.*

To Calman Pulowitz:

*First of all, what the hell do you want brothers and sisters
for? Jesus, you can have all of mine, that would be just fine
with me. I'd have my own room then and time to sit on the
toilet with the newspaper. You can't have my dog, though, he's
the only one I can tolerate (except for my grandfather). Larry's a*

Labrador retriever. He'll eat anything Lily cooks. One time I slipped him some of Lily's pureed peas to lick off my plate, but I didn't know that he'd finished everybody else's peas at the table, too (except for Lily's). Lily was psyched that everyone liked them so much until she found Larry puking up green all over the linoleum. (That reminds me, I'd sooner freeze in hell before I picked up my dog's crap. What if it's runny?)

Lily and Bob pitched in the egg and sperm that started me, but all the facts aren't in. For someone who drips babies like a leaky faucet, Lily's pretty stupid when it comes to sex. I bet she doesn't even like it. And I look nothing like either of them, thank God. Lily looks like Santa's better half. She's completely blimped out, probably from popping us out and sitting on her butt all day reading horndog novels. She's delusional, too. One of these days she's going to crack and it's not going to be pretty. Bob's harmless, even though he's six foot four and scary-looking. It helps to know where he's ticklish. He's a doctor. Need any Viagra?

I'm fourteen, and I'm the smartest one in my class. But that's not saying much. My classmates are a bunch of idiots, which is why I got picked to be a pen pal. I'm probably the only one who could spell my own name right.

So why would I ever have a reason to go to Boston? Were you ever in Walla Walla? We're known for our onions, you know. Everyone brags about how Walla Walla onions are so sweet and tasty. I think it's perfect that we're known for something that makes people cry. I cut up a few of those *suckers right before faking a temper tantrum, just for the effect.*

I have to go. Lily's going to want to read this letter before I send it, so I have to start writing a fake, sappy one to show her.

WBS (write back soon), Razor (aka Rizzy) Dickson

How Many Roads Must a Man Walk Down?

Calman met Mrs. Blenke because she sat next to him on the one-hour flight from the Seattle-Tacoma airport to Walla Walla. Calman found her adept at communicating large chunks of her life in short periods of time, and this comforted him. In fact, everything about her was comforting after a while. She wore pastels, smelled like pastels would smell, and had a voice like you'd find from an old lady knitting in a rocking chair, surrounded by flowered wallpaper.

"And what's your name, young man?"

Calman had been staring out over the wing when Mrs. Blenke accidentally swung her handbag into the side of his head. The conversation between them had thus begun with an apology.

"Calman," said Calman.

"Good afternoon. This is Captain John Harrington," bellowed the captain over the loudspeaker.

One of the flight attendants came around just then. "Could you fasten your seat belt for me, honey? We're about to pull back from the gate."

"Hmph," sighed Mrs. Blenke, "like that'd make a difference."

Calman felt a renewed wave of panic as the plane moved slowly in reverse. He had endured the miserable end-of-school parties, three emergency sessions with his therapist, and the bone-crunching hugs from his mother in the airport only to find himself sealed into a pressurized bubble about to engage in the unnatural act of flight.

Mrs. Blenke snapped open her barrette to free her soft, silver hair, and reached beneath the seat for her purse.

Calman watched her hands. They were swollen and crooked with age, yet moved gracefully to smooth in her rose-scented hand cream. "Because, you know, I hate to fly," she said, as if she were in the middle of a conversation. "I think my son, Oscar, knew I hated to fly when he moved to Walla Walla. He knew I hated to drive long ways, too. After his father died, he thought he'd get away from his mother by moving east. But I still visit." She pressed her seat back and yawned. "I guess he could've really moved away. Out of state, I mean. Oh, he loves me, I know that. And he needs me, even though he'd never dare admit it. Mothers always need to be needed." She paused and turned around to survey the back of the plane. "I always

turned to look at the wall, apologized for the disturbance, caught his falling knapsack, then stumbled for something to hold on to.

"Nice to meet you," said Sal, smiling.

Calman regained his balance and looked at Rizzy, then at Sal, and again at Rizzy. "You're Rizzy?" asked Calman with unbridled astonishment. He felt nauseous.

"Yeah," said Rizzy, suddenly scowling and poised for a fight. She leaned forward with her right hand on her hip. "You got a problem with that?"

Calman looked at Sal, who was still smiling pleasantly. "Well," said Calman, "it's just that I, I thought you were a boy."

"The hell I am," stormed Rizzy, flinging her arm in the air. The three adults opened the kitchen door to come inside just in time to see Rizzy grab the bottom edge of her dress and yank it up to her nose, exposing tight white panties.

"Look, Ma," she said mockingly, "no penis."

1 Feel So Break Up, 1 Want to Go Home

"Oh, my Lord!" Lily Dickson erupted at the sight of Rizzy's underwear. "Rosalita Dickson, pull down your dress, for God's sake . . . Jesus, Mary, and Joseph." She moved around the kitchen with dramatic gestures, performing a ritualistic dance of embarrassment. She initially turned away from Rizzy, placing her left hand on her rippling hip and her right hand over her eyes, head back, mouth open. Next she turned toward Calman and covered her mouth, then clutched her heart, breathed deeply, and fanned herself with her free hand, eyes closed. She finally took a step in one direction, a step in another, and repeated the set. "Such behavior," she exclaimed, "*in front of a guest!*"

Calman knew immediately who this frenzied woman was, thanks to the meticulous descriptions Rizzy had offered in her letters. There before him were Mrs. Dickson's plump ankles; her pale, blotchy skin creased like necklaces around her neck; her bobby pins that dangled from stray strands of thin blond hair piled high atop her head; and, above all, her high-pitched histrionics. Rizzy had described her as a Jekyll-and-Hyde type: sappy sweet and dainty-ladylike one minute, then hideous and beastly the next. Would he know which one was which?

Rizzy's siblings, who had scrambled through the kitchen and up the stairs so fast that they missed Calman's introduction, dropped their shovels on the second floor and ran back to see what it was that had riled Lily. Rizzy had let go of her dress at Lily's first command and was standing solidly in the corner with the shovel still upright in her left hand. She rolled her eyes several times, irritated by Lily's melodrama.

Calman turned his attention to the tall, stooped man with burgeoning sweat stains who he assumed was Rizzy's father by the way he put his arm around Lily's shoulders and encouraged her to calm down. Bob Dickson stood nearly a foot taller than Lily, which enabled her to nestle her cheek into the nook of his armpit. His face was long and chiseled and busy with large pores and pockmarks, but he radiated warmth with his sincere smile and soft, pale eyes.

The other adult in the room remained in the doorway, giggling beneath his bushy graying beard and matching gray tam-o'-shanter. Calman guessed he was the much-loved Simon McCory, Rizzy's grandfather.

"Will you please stop your snickering, Daddy? For God's

sake, I don't know what's so amusing." Lily patted her forehead with a damp washcloth and glowered at Rizzy's grandfather. "My Lord, I wish you wouldn't encourage her."

"What's so funny, Grandpa?" chirped a little girl from the fourth step. She stood with her dress in her hands so she wouldn't trip coming down the stairs.

"Never you mind, Francesca," yelled Lily over her shoulder. While Lily paced and Rizzy yelled and her grandfather chortled and two children quarreled, the one they called Francesca sauntered quietly over to Calman and stood in front of him. She rocked back and forth and looked up at him, biting her lip with the help of two fingers. Calman noticed, of all things, that the part in her hair was crooked.

"I'm Francesca. I'm four. Who are you?"

Calman stood tightly still amid the pandemonium.

Rizzy's father turned to the bickering children behind him and patted the air. "Shh," he whispered, "that's enough, children." Then he turned back to Calman and smiled. The rest of the Dicksons quieted down, and for a brief moment they stared at Calman as he'd seen them stare at the new mound of dirt in the backyard. The silence was as stifling as the dry desert heat. The air in the kitchen smelled like a slightly rancid blend of old food and perspiration.

"This is Calman," said Sal. "He's Rizzy's friend." Sal walked over to Calman and tossed Calman's knapsack over his shoulder. Calman's gratitude for Sal's interruption and comforting smile nearly reached the limits of love. "I'll take your bags up-

of *National Geographic*, "I never saw anyone faint. For real, I mean."

"It's no big deal. I've fainted before," said Calman, who meant simply to state a fact rather than brag. He was beginning to feel stronger and a little more at ease, although he was very conscious of the fact that it was Rizzy's bed he was lying on and that Rizzy, after all, was a girl. He wondered where Sal had disappeared to.

"You dropped to the floor like one of those houses you make out of playing cards. How'd you do that?"

"I don't know. I never really thought about it, I guess." The last time Calman had fainted was during gym class when James O'Grady accidentally socked him in the groin with a Wiffle bat. James O'Grady thought he should have gotten at least two bases for hitting "the ball" straight down the middle. Calman thought James O'Grady had a serious humor deficiency.

As Calman was remembering the shooting pain, Rizzy stood up suddenly and, with exaggerated gestures, twirled about, rolled her neck, fanned herself, fluttered her eyelids, sighed a few times, and gradually collapsed into a heap in the middle of the floor. She remained on the floor for a moment with her arms by her sides, presumably for dramatic emphasis. Calman was stunned.

"How was that?" asked Rizzy, assembling her limp body into a standing position like a puppet on strings.

"Did I look like that when I fainted?" asked Calman, ready for another exhausting rush of humiliation.

"No, of course not. That's how they do it in old movies."

"Oh. I guess it was pretty good, then."

Rizzy leaned against her desk. "I do a 'pretty good' death scene, too. Wanna see?"

"Sure," said Calman.

"You'll have to shoot me." Rizzy stood and waited for a gunshot.

Calman, a little unsure of how to execute a murder, pointed two fingers at Rizzy and cocked his thumb. "Bang," he said.

"You call that a shooting?" said Rizzy.

Calman tried to imagine the noise guns made in gangster movies or video games and ended up firing a continuous stream of guttural bullets and spit in Rizzy's direction.

Rizzy took more time dying than she did fainting. She clutched her heart, bounced off her bed, and groped for her desk chair only to miss its edge and fall in agony to the floor, one joint at a time. She lay sprawled out on the carpet with her eyes crossed, tongue out, lungs gasping for last little bits of air.

There they remained—Calman stretched out and sweaty on Rizzy's bed, and Rizzy twitching in the imaginary throes of death below him—when Sal walked in and, having seen Rizzy's performance before, played along by calling out Rizzy's name and wiping invisible tears from his cheeks. He rushed to her side and knelt down close to her face.

"Salvador? Is that you?" breathed Rizzy. She took his hand in hers as a parting gesture. She seemed thrilled to have Sal in a supporting role.

"Yeah, Riz. It's me."

"Sal, my brother. Get me a cigarette."

Sal reached behind for a pencil and stuck the back end in his mouth. He lit it with his thumbnail behind his cupped palm, and blew invisible smoke rings at Calman. He transferred it to Rizzy's twisted mouth. "Riz?" he said, watching Rizzy inhale with sunken cheeks. It looked to Calman as if she might swallow it.

"Yeah, Sal. What is it?" coughed Rizzy.

"Don't you worry about being dead. I'll make sure Dad stuffs you so you're sittin' pretty with your lips all ready for kissing in case Roland Gates comes calling."

"Oh, gross!" yelled Rizzy, now alive and kicking. Sal fell backward in a ball of laughter. He explained to Calman that Roland Gates was a thirteen-year-old neighbor of theirs who had the misfortune of having a crush on Rizzy. His contagious giggles penetrated Calman and finally Rizzy, too, once she found the humor in thinking of Roland Gates being all excited about kissing a corpse.

"Can't you just see that lard-butt trying to stick his tongue down my dead throat?!" she howled. Rizzy's acting reminded Calman of Mrs. Blenke's husband with his face in a plate of summer squash. For some reason, death had never been so funny as it was on this day.

The three of them laughing made enough noise to reach the kitchen.

"Rosalita, what's going on up there?" yelled Lily.

They exchanged glances and slowly quieted down until the only noise Calman could hear came from Rizzy's siblings outside. They had come into the house to wash up after the funeral only to run back outside to get dirty trying to cross the "Robert Dickson" line. "Crossing the Robert Dickson line" was a game Rizzy's father had thought up, explained Rizzy. The object was to run up to him, touch him, and try to leap over, duck under, or simply get past him any way you could. Dr. Dickson said he loved the game because, according to his rules, he had to be lying down in a lawn chair at all times.

There was an awkward silence in Rizzy's room now. The fan sputtered for a moment as if the air was too thick with tension to spin. Rizzy, pensive and somewhat distant, sat with her head low and drew lines in the carpet with her finger. Sal was intent on unraveling paper clips he had found on Rizzy's desk. "What's in your mind?" Calman could hear his therapist ask, as he always did during heavy silences like this. Other therapists asked what was "on" your mind, but it was really about what's "in" your mind, said his therapist. His parents paid extra for details like that. *I'm just sorry about their dog.* That's what was really "in" his mind, as sincere and as simple as a hug. He knew how much Larry meant to Rizzy from her letters. But Calman had always had trouble matching his sentiments with his voice.

"Well," said Rizzy as she stood and made her way to the door. "You should probably rest until dinner, Cal. Can I call you Cal?"

"Sure," said Calman, trying to be cheerful. He liked the

head to tip it into a Dumpster. His own mother handed all jars over to his father without even making an attempt to open them herself. Calman had watched the jiggly flesh under Lily's arms harden under the trash can's weight, and he thought about how odd it was that you sometimes didn't know how strong people could be from their appearance.

"Hey, Cal. Did you know my grandfather can stick his whole index finger up his nose?" asked Rizzy as she sat down with her second helping.

"No," said Calman, a little unsure if she was challenging his intelligence. Calman fell for tricks and jokes much more often than he would have liked.

"Show him, Grandpa," she said, at which Simon nodded and giggled and turned away.

He tilted his head back a few times as if he was indeed stuffing something up his nose, and when he turned back toward them, Calman was astonished. His index finger couldn't have been bent or hidden, since his hand was flat against his face. There was nowhere for his finger to go except up his left nostril.

"How does he do that?" asked Calman, unconsciously pinching his nose shut.

"Watch him take it out. It'll be all covered in snot," said Rizzy.

"Rizzy, please, we're eating," said Lily behind her. "Dad, you know I hate when you do that."

"Lily, you hush now," said Simon, as he lowered his hand

from his face to point at her with the finger that had been in his nose. That was when Calman noticed his finger was missing! Calman nearly choked on his corn bread. Simon had been sticking his phantom finger up his nose and pointing it at people ever since he had lost the fleshy one to frostbite, he explained.

Rizzy loved the nose-picking trick. She said she might have cut off her own finger if the trick hadn't already been done. "You got something unique, you milk it for all it's worth," said Rizzy's grandfather.

"*Enough!*" screamed Lily abruptly. "Just *shut up* for once." They all stopped what they were doing and looked at her. She had slammed a metal plate on the table and caused a fork to somersault into the bowl of pickles. Calman didn't dare move his jaw to finish chewing. Lily pressed down air with her palms and breathed deeply. "I hate when you do that, Daddy, it's disgusting. And for God's sake, you just let me do the teaching for once. They're *my* children."

Despite his afternoon attempts to relax, Calman was still tired and a little woozy from the day's spent energy. After supper, the children didn't go in and play video games or watch TV; they stayed outside and played jacks or Pick Up Sticks, or just sat, digesting, saying something funny when it came to mind. It made Calman uncomfortable. Plus, he had a good view of the mound of dirt where they had buried Larry. It was distracting. The mound protruded from the ground and imbued Calman's imagination with darkness and fears of death and the unknown.

"Cal, you with us?" Rizzy asked more than once that night.

When the moon ended the day with a soft glimmer, Lily coaxed the younger Dicksons up to bed. Bob had fallen asleep in the lawn chair that Simon had fallen asleep in shortly after dinner. Simon had snored himself awake and had strolled back to his trailer for what he called "a little night music."

"What's your grandfather doing?" asked Calman, looking toward the open door of the trailer.

"He's playing the banjo," said Rizzy. "Haven't you seen a banjo before?"

"Sure," said Calman hesitantly.

Rizzy and Calman snuck up to the window around back and peered under the curtains. The contents of the trailer were divided, so it seemed, into piles and clusters: piles of laundry and papers and books and clusters of toiletries and dishes and yellowed house plants. Crayon drawings addressed to "Grandpa" hung on the far wall, creating a jagged frame for a *Playboy* calendar, stuck on the month of January. It was the kind of mess that would have sent his mother into a coma. Simon sat upright, wearing a torn undershirt and boxer shorts. The round part of the banjo rested on his lap; his left arm was wrapped around the neck. Calman watched the hand with the missing finger. The other fingers seemed to compensate for its absence, moving strangely and yet somehow skillfully across the wire strings. Simon was singing with his eyes closed:

I've been having some hard traveling, I thought you knowed,
I've been having some hard traveling, way down the road,
I've been having some hard traveling, hard rambling, hard gambling,
Been a having some hard traveling, Lord . . .

Simon's voice slid over the notes with soft, melancholy words. Calman listened and felt soothed, and a little sad. He watched Simon's lips move, his bearded chin jut out now and again, and his eyes flutter under his lids, beneath his gray tam-o'-shanter. How different this music was from what his parents played at home. His mother liked to put classical music on in the background when she cleaned or did a crossword puzzle; his father put it on when he paid the bills or searched the Internet. It was pretty music, but it didn't have lyrics, and his parents never *listened* to it, could never tell him what the name of the piece was exactly, or why it was so popular. He'd hear the same music in the accountant's office or in the nurse's office at school, and it would make him sleepy. But he felt Simon's music deeply. It conjured up images in his mind of poor lonely ragged old men with stories to share. It made him feel part of a collective sorrow, and this somehow comforted him.

"Rizzy?" Lily crooned from the house. "Where are you, dear? It's time for bed."

Rizzy glanced at Calman and rolled her eyes.

Calman thought maybe he'd like a grandfather like Simon McCory, someone with a messy home, a gentle voice, and a missing finger, someone who didn't have anything to be up-tight about.

"My grandfather says he's the best nine-fingered banjo player in the world," said Rizzy.

Calman followed Rizzy to the house, imagining a field full of nine-fingered banjo players and Simon up front with a large medal around his neck. Wouldn't it be nice, thought Calman, to be *best* at something.

Sal was in bed when Calman finished brushing his teeth. Sal's brothers in the same room were asleep. The house was nearly as quiet as it had been the moment Calman had entered it for the first time, which, although it was just hours before, already seemed a distant memory. Calman imagined Mrs. Blenke sleeping in a guest room and Oscar huddled over some paperwork under a circle of dim lamplight. He wondered if he would ever see Mrs. Blenke again. In the quiet of night, he sort of missed her.

"Do you pray before you go to sleep, Cal?" whispered Sal over the top of his pillow. Their beds lay side by side, only Cal-man's cot was a little lower to the ground.

"No, not really," said Calman, somehow thrilled by the inti-macy of their conversation. "I mean, sometimes I do, but it's not anything formal. Do you?"

"No. I figure if everybody else does it before bed, God already has an earful. I just pray on my own time."

"What do you pray for?" asked Calman. He was flat on his back, staring up at the cracks in the ceiling. He wasn't at all convinced that there was anyone out there who would want to listen to his requests.

"I don't know. The usual, I guess. Peace on earth, all that stuff. Though, come Christmas, I fit a lot more praying in for things I can ride or throw around instead of things I have to wear. I don't know who's got worse taste, Mom or Dad."

"My parents usually give me money for Hanukkah," said Calman. That, and eight token gifts. His parents sometimes found it funny to wrap just one shoe or one glove as a gift, which would ruin the surprise for the next night.

"That'd be great," said Sal. "You get to buy anything you want?"

"No. They make me put it into savings." He never really got to see the money. It was all written out on a check and deposited without even a trace of Calman's fingerprints.

"What for?" asked Sal.

"College, I guess," said Calman. "Or maybe for when I'm old, like my grandmother."

"I don't like thinking about getting old," said Sal. Calman didn't answer. Thoughts of old age led to thoughts of death, and that was a subject neither one of them had the energy to discuss.

Calman lay there quietly, listening to the rhythmic breathing of Sal's three younger brothers. Fabio, Brock, and Ricardo—those were their names. Asleep, they looked angelic, but in the waking hours they were a mischievous trio at the ages of seven, nine, and eleven. That afternoon they had been shooting at each other, running around the house with flashing, blasting futuristic toy megaweapons. They went everywhere together, did everything together; "would pee together if any of them could make it into the toilet bowl," Rizzy had said.

Sal said good night and turned over toward the wall. It almost felt to Calman that they were sleeping in the same bed. He had a strange urge to touch Sal. Just his shoulder, or the wisps of hair that reflected the glow of the moon through the window. Calman couldn't sleep. He was tired but restless, and annoyed that thoughts of his therapist kept weaving their way into his mind. He'd been seeing his therapist once a week since he was seven years old, or roughly from the time his parents assumed he was old enough to gain a basic understanding of the therapeutic process. Though the number of psychosomatic illnesses Calman suffered from had doubled since his first therapy session, he had learned to accept the blame for their existence. Minimizing them through meditation, however, proved more difficult, but he and his therapist were working on that. Calman had homework assignments, one of which was an exercise on "focusing" his attention to cure his insomnia, which he tried now, lying on his side facing Sal.

At least a hundred minutes and thousands of seconds passed before Calman ran out of things to count. He'd given up on sleeping by now and was beginning to think he wouldn't make it through the night without throwing up. He knew his stomach wasn't asleep. He could hear it.

He sat up very slowly, got out of bed, and tiptoed over to his suitcase, stopping after each creak he made to listen for any movement from the surrounding beds. His eyes had had plenty of time to adjust to the dark, but he didn't want to wake anyone. Besides, he had all night.

He unzipped his suitcase, one notch at a time, and searched through its contents until he found the Pepto-Bismol, which he was appalled to find was nearly empty. He had packed a second bottle, but it was in the first-aid kit that he had left on the backseat of Oscar's car. He dug around some more and found the Swiss Army Knife that Cousin Shirley had given him for his bar mitzvah. He liked having it with him and thought it was a good idea image-wise to carry a knife when visiting a bully, seeing as he was also carrying floral packets of tissues and pink stomach medicine. He had hidden it in his suitcase despite his mother's warning that it wasn't a good idea to take anything like that on the plane.

The knife made him think of his parents. He had used the Dicksons' phone earlier to call his mother's cell phone and let them know he arrived safely, but they were already on their way to Florida. His message said that he had taken all necessary precautions on the plane against infection from recirculated air and exposure to cosmic radiation, and though his back felt strained from prolonged inactivity, he was sure he'd be just fine now that he was on terra firma, so no worries.

Thinking of his parents made him homesick. He was sure now that his stomach was getting ready to reject the baby back ribs. He had to find a bathroom.

The brothers and sisters in the Dickson household had separate bathrooms, and although he'd been in the boys' bathroom to wash up before bed, he forgot his way and took a wrong turn at the end of the hallway. The girls' bathroom looked just like Rizzy's bedroom. There were words from various magazines and newspapers taped everywhere except in the shower. He couldn't find the main light switch, so he moved aside the wicker wastepaper basket to get the full shine from the butterfly night-light. He lifted up the lid of the toilet toward a sign directly above it that read DUMPING GROUNDS. The bathroom door didn't shut properly, and he had trouble keeping it from swinging open. It was quiet enough to hear himself pull down his pajama bottoms and pull off sheets of toilet paper to line the toilet seat before he sat down. He was feeling a little better now that he was in the proper place should he have to empty his bowels, but he didn't want to take any chances. He thought perhaps the girls kept some of their own Pepto-Bismol in the medicine cabinet behind the mirror. He could reach it over the sink from where he sat. He popped open the mirrored door, *whoosh*, hundreds of bouncing glass marbles came pouring out into the night, crashing into the sink and onto the cold floor tiles, where they pierced the silence like a sudden downpour of hail against a tin roof, and in no time at all scattered into the hallway.

"*Oh, my Lord.* Bob, get up," Calman heard. Lily came running out of her bedroom in a low-cut white cotton nightie and turned the bend toward the bathroom. The floor rolled underneath her feet, and as she groped for the wall, the stray marbles flipped her up and dumped her with a thump on her rear end. If the avalanche in the bathroom had awakened the rest of the Dicksons from sleep, Lily's fall coaxed them out of bed and into the hallway to see what was happening.

"Lily, my goodness, are you all right?" asked Bob, flicking on the lights. Clumps of his hair were vertical.

"Mama, what are you doing on the floor?" asked Francesca, rubbing her eyes.

Lily got up with Bob's help and stared at the floor. With one hand, she rubbed her large rear end where a sizable black-and-blue mark was sure to form, and covered her semi-exposed bosom with the other hand, seemingly out of habit.

"Where did all these marbles come from?" asked Bob, watching the trio of boys collecting them in their fists.

"And where's Calman?" asked Sal, who was the last one out of his room.

At the sound of his name, Calman emerged from the girls' bathroom at the end of the hall with his hand over his heart.

"I'm sorry," he said, trembling and somewhat out of breath.

"I . . . I was just looking for Pepto-Bismol. They . . . they fell out of the medicine cabinet."

"What were they doing in the medicine cabinet?" yelled Lily.

Calman shrugged and looked around for Rizzy, hoping that she hadn't seen anything. Amid the marbles at his feet were other medicine cabinet regulars—a box of Q-tips, dental floss, sparkly tubes of toothpaste, and some sort of green packet which by accident he kicked over to the tips of Lily's toes.

"Those are birth control pills," said Bob, looking over Lily's shoulder as she picked up the green packet and opened it. "How'd that get in the girls' bathroom?"

"No way!" said Sal with a smile. "Are they Rizzy's?"

"They are most certainly *not* Rizzy's," said Lily, hiding them behind her back.

"I bet they are," sang Sal.

"Quiet!"

"Lily," said Bob. "Honey, they look like your pills. How did Rizzy get them?"

"Shh. I don't know, Robert," whispered Lily, pushing him aside.

"Rizzy's getting some!" Sal yelled out.

"That's enough! Robert, help me with these marbles. Every-one else, back to bed!"

Calman's stomach still hurt, but all he wanted to do was get under his covers.

"Look," whispered Sal, motioning Calman to peek into Rizzy's bedroom. Rizzy was in bed with her eyes closed. She had her Walkman on.

"So she didn't hear any of that, you think?" Calman whispered.

"Oh, she heard," said Sal, as they all slid back into bed.

Hang Your Head Over, Hear the Wind Blow

The long, unbearably hot and dry summer days in Walla Walla were often treated like events by storefront conversationalists. "Can you believe . . ." some would start, referring to global warming or the greenhouse effect or the price of sunscreen. And this particular summer, the older citizens commented, was hotter than it had been in years.

The incident involving the marbles became another favorite topic of conversation among neighbors, thanks to Simon McCory, who, upon hearing the story the following morning, removed his cap and shook with laughter, then shared the story with the breakfast crowd at the local diner.

"My granddaughter, God love her, says to her screaming mother, 'Well, nobody's supposed to look in a girl's medicine cabinet. It's a personal thing.' Hoo-wee. Did her mother have a fit."

The Saturday morning breakfast crowd that appraised Calman with practiced side-glances had changed very little in twenty years. Rizzy's grandfather said that the same few were there when the diner opened each morning and were gone before the restaurant filled with what he called the "irregular" customers. The others in the group came with stories—sometimes true, sometimes not—about their grandchildren scoring points, winning fights, and getting high marks at school. Simon came with stories about pranks and women. The better stories, he said, involved both. Calman listened to Simon with his eyes on his lap and his mind forcibly focused on a crinkled napkin so as to avoid reliving the marble incident in the telling. Rizzy was in the bathroom.

"Simon, that girl's fourteen years old," said the waitress, who smelled like Vicks VapoRub. She replenished his coffee across the counter and removed his plate. "What she doing with birth control?"

"Gettin' Lily's goat, is what she's doing. Poor Lily. That woman trails trouble like a shadow. She's gonna get a big ol' bruise on that there rump of hers." Simon's listeners swiveled in their seats and giggled into their sausages and hash browns.

"Shoot, that child can make my sides ache," said Simon as he adjusted his hat. "Calman, my boy, you're in for one heck of a ride."

Calman sipped his orange juice and wiped his lips with his

paper napkin before he placed it back neatly on his lap. Remembering what was in the front pocket of his shorts, he removed a plastic bag of vitamins. He slid some of them into his palm, and from there placed them in a row in front of his bowl. One by one, he dropped them into his oatmeal and, with his spoon, mixed his oatmeal until the pills were hidden. He put a spoonful into his mouth, followed by a big swig from his water glass, and swallowed dutifully.

"What you doing there, son?" said Simon.

Calman looked up and noticed he was being watched. Simon, the waitress, and two of the people sitting near Calman were eyeing his vitamin concoction.

"Um, nothing."

"You taking pills?" said the waitress.

"No. They're dietary supplements. This one," he said, exposing a small white pill from his plastic bag, "is vitamin C to ward off colds, which are easy to catch when you're in a foreign place. This one is vitamin B for stress. This one is calcium to help me get strong bones because osteoporosis runs in my family and even though it's more common in women, it's always good to be safe, and there's also vitamin D, I think, but I forget what it's for. I'm supposed to take these once a day with a meal and lots of water."

"Your mother give all that to you?" asked Simon.

Calman nodded.

"Why don't you just take one pill with all that stuff in it?" asked one of the nearby customers.

"I've tried, but it's too big. I can't swallow it."

"Sugar, no offense, but something tells me your mother's probably making you swallow a lot more than these here pills."

The people around Calman found that amusing. Though he didn't exactly understand the waitress's comment, he got the feeling that these people felt sorry for him, that somehow through his taking of vitamins they could tell just what his life was like, and this made him feel both defensive and angry that the habits he learned from his mother should be so odd and humiliating away from home. He pushed the plate of oatmeal aside.

"You going to eat that?" asked Rizzy upon her return from the bathroom. She nodded in the direction of Calman's oatmeal.

Calman looked at her. He couldn't figure her out. He wanted to ask her about the night before—about the marbles and even about birth control—but she'd made it pretty clear she didn't want to talk about it, especially not after all the yelling between her and her mother. Had it been a simple practical joke that got blown out of proportion? She didn't exactly laugh at him, as practical jokers do. Calman was sure at first that he was meant to be the victim of the joke, but now he wondered about that. Maybe he was more like the cue ball in this game of pool. He had lost his appetite. He wanted to go home. "No," he said, "I'm not hungry anymore."

"Good, pass the bowl over here, I'm still hungry."

———

To Calman's amazement, the Dicksons viewed the mound of dirt under which Larry lay buried not as a sacred place of unmentionable history but rather as a focal point for new games and I-remember-when discussions. It was only yesterday that Calman had seen them gathered around the mound with melancholy stares in an eerie silence, and now the kids were using the grave as home plate.

Calman had learned by his family's example to greet death as if it were royalty. You wore your best suit, bowed your head often, and tried to imagine what it would be like to experience it. That's how Calman remembered the Jewish Orthodox funeral of his Uncle Abraham. People spoke in low, monotone voices and stared at their socks, and afterward sat in a dark living room on stools and sipped tea. "Go ahead and cry if you need to," his mother had said. But crying was not what Calman had had in mind as he walked around the dark and gloomy interior of his cousin's third-floor walk-up. All he could remember of Uncle Abraham was that he cheated at Monopoly.

That was death, or "a death in the family": polite, awkward, and infrequent. There was also another kind of death that Calman knew of, the kind that took away your parents or your grandmother in the middle of the night. That was a haunting and elusive death whose possibility made him excruciatingly dizzy and choked him until he awoke. It would send him running into his parents' room, under their covers, between their warm bodies, and even then it lingered overhead until daybreak.

Either way, death was something Calman thought should be left alone. So when Rizzy explained the rules of the pedestal game—how you had to stand on the mound and declare, "I swear on Larry's grave that I will not," and then say what exactly you wouldn't do while everyone else tried to make you do what you said you wouldn't—Calman said he didn't want any part of it. He had visions of sinking into the dirt and being surrounded by Larry's decomposing remains, or worse, being haunted by ghosts for his irreverence.

"I'll just watch," he said, and he sat down and crossed his legs in a yoga position. His hands were busy picking individual blades of grass and trying to split them down the middle.

"Hogwash," said Rizzy. "Stop being such a sissy."

Calman offered to "just watch" in school any time the activity in question required more physical exertion than daydreaming. It was never a problem; no one had ever argued with Calman when he made such a decision, nor had anyone ever noticed his absence. He wasn't very good at playing sports or dancing or acting, and he was more often than not plagued with some sort of illness that no other classmate of his was willing to contract. So he had become adept at blending in with his environment.

But here in the Dickson household he was beginning to sense that things were going to be different. He ground his teeth at the thought.

"Everybody plays, or nobody plays. That's the rule."

A clearing had formed through the kids, so that Calman

could see Rizzy from where he sat. She was standing on "the pedestal" in cutoff jeans with her hands on her hips and a small stick in her left hand. She was clearly in charge and unwilling to put up with dissenters.

"Come on, Calman," said little Francesca, who had weaved her way past her siblings to stand next to him. She bent down and rested her palms on her knees as Calman had seen Francesca's father do when he needed to address her. "I'll hold your hand," she said. "We all have to hold hands first to seal the deal."

Calman looked at Francesca and then, as if possessed by some unknown force, he stood and said, "Okay." She slipped her hand into his, he looked at her, and the two of them walked over to the mound.

"Good," said Rizzy. "Now everyone grab hands, I'm making my declaration."

Calman had an odd sensation that his hands were suddenly acting of their own accord, for when he looked right he saw his hand was palm down and cupped over Francesca's delicate little fingers and she was using it to scratch her nose, and when he looked left he saw how snug and secure his hand, palm up, looked in Sal's grasp. Calman had recoiled at first from Sal's touch, from a boy's touch, but Sal—confidently and nonchalantly—held firm. His fingers were long and lean and calloused at the tips, and Calman liked how they grabbed hold and pressed against his knuckles. A palm-reading friend of his mother had told him once of his Life line and Heart line and there they were, pressed against Sal's Life line and Heart line. For the first time, he thought, he was holding the hand of someone other than his mother or father. His arms felt like wings.

"I swear on Larry's grave that on this day my palms will never touch the ground," yelled Rizzy. All six children encircled Rizzy and stretched their arms out to ensure that all hands were touching. She waved her stick in the air. "Done," she said.

The group suddenly hollered and danced around Rizzy like a pack of hungry wolves, for the rule was they couldn't touch Rizzy until she stepped off the mound. Rizzy, meanwhile, had taken a pair of mittens out of the back pocket of her jeans and was putting them on her hands.

"That's cheating," yelled Sal.

"No it's not," said Rizzy, and with that she bolted off the mound toward the back of Simon's trailer with a bunch of screaming kids in tow.

Calman tried his best to keep up. They chased Rizzy across the driveway, around the house, halfway down the gravel road, and over the neighbor's fence, into an onion field. Moments later, they were back at the house and had tackled her to the ground. Calman nearly lost his glasses in the jumble of flailing arms and kicking feet.

"I got her!" yelled Sal. "Get her mitten. *Calman, get it off!"*

Rizzy had clenched her mitten in her fist and had somehow

managed to lodge her left arm under Calman's armpit. That gave him easiest access. At Sal's command, he peeled the mitten past her knuckles and, to the chanting of "down, down, down," forced her hand to the ground. There were cheers, and then Rizzy let out a piercing wail.

"*Ow!* I'm hurt. *I'm hurt!* Calman, *you hurt me!*" Rizzy rose to her feet. She was clutching her crotch and pointing at Calman accusingly.

Calman's heart throbbed with sudden guilt and astonishment. He had never hurt anyone before.

"Oh, my God," said Rizzy. She had stuck her hand down her shorts and was now staring at her fingers. *"Blood. I'm bleeding!"*

"Oh, my Lord," yelled Lily as she swung open the kitchen door. "What's going on? Who's hurt?" She was wiping her hands in the folds of her apron.

"Calman hurt Rizzy, Calman hurt Rizzy," sang Francesca.

Lily pushed Rizzy's brothers aside and stared down at Rizzy. "What happened to you?"

"I'm bleeding." Lily gave her a suspicious look.

"Where?"

"My vagina." Rizzy's siblings burst into sudden laughter.

"Ooh, Rizzy said a dirty word, Mama," said Francesca, who was giggling behind her cupped hands.

"Rosalita, that's not amusing," said Lily, who was looking at Rizzy in a peculiar way. "That's enough now. Get inside."

"What did I do? Say 'vagina'? It's just a word."

"For God's sake, just once I'd like to see you act like a proper young lady."

"Oh, like you? That's a laugh."

"How dare you!" Lily heaved with rage, and with every deep inhalation the strings of her apron emerged from beneath the rolls of her waistline and then receded. In a light gray house-dress, she looked a little like Silly Putty around the middle, but she stood like a bull with her head jutting forward and her nostrils slightly flared. She was definitely at a Level Ten anger, as his therapist would call it. During Calman's sessions, his therapist insisted that Calman rate his anger on a scale of one to ten when he couldn't find the precise vocabulary for description. Calman had never given himself above a five. Lily grabbed Rizzy by the wrist, but Rizzy yanked her arm up and away in backstroke fashion and ran into the house. Lily looked down toward the ground at Calman, who felt compelled to rise and apologize for the skirmishes of the day, or at least to say something, for surely she was looking at him as if he should say *something*, but instead she took a Tootsie Roll from her pocket, unwrapped it, popped it into her mouth, closed her eyes, took a deep breath, steadied herself into Dr. Jekyll again, opened her eyes, turned to Calman before she walked away, and said, "I'm sorry for my daughter's behavior."

Calman sat down at the end of the picnic table. He was shaking—from fear, surely—but he felt angry, too, and didn't know why or at whom. He had that faint sense again—one he'd felt many times before—that time and space were twirling tornado-style around the roots of a deepfelt anger. *I'm sorry for my son's behavior. He's currently seeing a therapist. My husband and I are doing what we can. I'm sorry. I'm really very sorry.*

"You okay?" asked Sal, who had taken a seat next to Calman. Sal's siblings had already found another activity to keep themselves occupied.

Calman thought he had accidentally kneed Rizzy in her lower abdomen during the skirmish. He thought he had seen her wince. It was as quick as a flicker, but it was for real, it seemed. "I think I may have really hurt Rizzy."

"Oh, she'll be okay. She did the same thing to me last month. She thinks it's funny."

"What's funny?"

"You know, to blame us for her period. She started getting it a few months ago."

Calman was eight years old when his mother showed him a tampon and explained *the beautiful and natural act* of menstruation and the misconceptions about premenstrual moods, *which your father has no right to use as an excuse when he wants to dismiss me. For God's sake don't you be like him, Calman, you be a sensitive man and celebrate the female body.*

"She's been going to this special doctor, not like Dad," continued Sal. "A girl doctor. I don't think she's too happy about the whole thing. Means she has to admit she really is a girl."

"Is she okay, though? Maybe it's painful for her."

"C'mon, Rizzy? She's fine. Look at her. She can beat us

both up with one fist. Anyway," said Sal, "you won. Rizzy's gotta be mad. She hates to lose."

"I'm sorry I won."

"That's stupid. I'm glad you won. She deserves it."

"Still . . . your mom looked pretty mad."

"Yeah, but that's nothing new. She and Rizzy don't get along very well."

"How come?"

"I don't know. It's like Rizzy's got rabies or something. She snarls at everyone, but mostly at my mother. It wasn't always like that, though. Before we moved to this house a few years ago, Rizzy was fun to be around, always laughing and stuff. Fact, she was my mom's favorite. She even let my mom dress her up like a real girl, show her off, you know. But she changed. Something changed. Anyway, it's no use trying to figure her out. I'm going in the house, it's too hot out here."

Calman drank a tall glass of homemade peach iced tea in the late afternoon.

"Calman, dear," said Lily as she stood over him and refilled his glass. It was just the two of them in the kitchen. "Your mother called while you were out. She said they were doing something or other, I can't really remember, but she'd call again tomorrow. I told her everything was just fine, that you were having a good time running around outside with the children." She put the pitcher down and wiped a spot on the table. "Your mother seemed surprised by that. Don't you run around out-side with the children at home?"

"Not really," said Calman. He looked down at his lap. He wished he hadn't missed his mother's call.

"Well, I'm sure whatever it is you boys do back East is very fun, all the same. Oh, and she said to tell you that she and your father love you very much." Lily stopped moving about and looked at Calman warmly. "That's nice that they say that," she said softly in a half-compliment, half-realization sort of way. For a moment she looked at nothing in particular out the screen door, contemplating. Then she sat down at the other end of the table and went back to her book, which had the words "Loveswept" and "Scandal" written on the cover in curly letters above half-dressed, windblown models with wistful stares and sweaty skin. She took out her bookmark, which Cal-man saw was a torn picture of her younger self with her arm around a life-size photograph of Elvis Presley. Elvis had obvi-ously been cut out, pasted on wood, and propped up for the benefit of tourists. Across the top of the picture it read "A Dream Come True." Lily sat at the kitchen table with her fist pressed to her bosom.

She didn't seem so monstrous now, thought Calman. He certainly couldn't imagine her biting the heads off chickens like Rizzy said she did, even if she was Mr. Hyde. Maybe Rizzy just lied a lot. "Good book, Mrs. Dickson?"

Lily offered a small sigh without looking up and said, "Mmm, that's nice, dear," and turned the page.

He walked tentatively to the bottom of the stairs. Rizzy was up there, in her room. He could hear her typing. He thought he should say something to her, that he was sorry he'd touched her, that he himself had been touched in his private area many times by his doctor and his neighbor's poodle, for example, and so he knew how awkward it could be. But he didn't have the energy. And maybe, he thought, she was typing a letter to another pen pal. Perhaps he had failed the pen pal trial period and she was seeking his replacement, this time a girl who understood what she needed in a friend. Must be fun and adventurous and smart, was probably what the clack-clack-clacking was printing on the page. If you're boring and have chronic acid indigestion, don't call us, we'll call you.

Calman walked into the TV room and sat down on the couch next to Francesca.

"I'm watching *Beauty and the Beast*," said Francesca. "I've seen it a million times." She poked her tongue into her cheek and stretched her shirt over her knees.

"You must like it."

Francesca giggled and rocked in her seat. "Am I hot? Feel my forehead. Mama says I'm hot, maybe I'm sick." She grabbed his hand and pressed it against her forehead.

"You feel okay," said Calman. "Where is everyone? It's quiet around here."

"It's alone time."

"What is that?"

"It's when everyone gets to be alone. Mama says we all need our alone time or else we'll go crazy."

Alone time. Somehow he had heard that phrase before. Calman thought for a moment, and remembered that it was Mrs. Blenke who said she liked her alone time. Calman leaned back against the couch and tried to imagine what it was like to *want* to be alone.

You hate being alone, don't you, Calman.

No.

You're angry that your parents aren't home a lot.

No.

Your mother tells me you've taken to calling a 900 number. Some sort of psychic hotline.

No.

What do you ask them, Calman?

Nothing.

Are you concerned about your future?

No.

Is it just someone to talk to? Who will listen? I'm listening to you, Calman. That's what I do best. I'm a therapist, remember. What do you want to say to me Calman? What do you want to say to me?

I wish you would all leave me alone.

"Calman."

"Yeah."

"You're not supposed to be with me right now."

"Oh. Do you want me to leave?"

"No, it's okay. You're new, and you didn't know. But if I start going crazy, you'll have to leave the room."

Calman felt an affection for Francesca. He liked being with her, liked that she liked being with him.

"Calman, do you eat mushrooms?"

"They're okay."

Francesca fidgeted with her shirt. She took her arms out of the sleeves and turned the V-neck to the back. "They grow in dirt, you know, and they're brown like doodie."

A discussion of mushrooms, thought Calman, was better than silence, even if it included the word "doodie." Discussions between two people about fainting and fingers and husbands that fake their own deaths and God were better, to be sure, than the festering thoughts in one person's head about one's infinite inadequacies.

"Francesca, can I ask you a question?"

"Okay." Francesca slid down the couch headfirst and somersaulted onto the carpet.

"What do you think about when you're alone?"

"What?"

"I said," said Calman, leaning toward her, "what do you think about when you're alone?"

Francesca jumped up on her toes and twirled and giggled and made herself dizzy. "I think about doodie. Doodie doodie doodie!" She jumped back onto the couch and emitted a substantial fart for a girl her size and shrieked with pleasure. That made Calman laugh, too, and they both laughed, the two of them, until the laughter ran its course and they were out of breath. Then it was quiet except for the singing teapot on TV.

"What are you two losers doing?" said Rizzy, joining them in the TV room. She looked tough. She wore a blue bandanna tight around the top of her head, and she held the neck of a brown bottle in her fist. It looked like beer, but Calman knew it was just root beer because earlier her mother had offered him some, too.

"Hi, Rizzy," said Francesca, without taking her eyes off the screen. "Want to watch with us? Belle's in the castle. Look."

Rizzy walked over to the TV and shut it off.

"Hey," Francesca whined.

"Francesca, you watch too much TV. What happened to reading? Where are your books?"

"I don't want to read."

Rizzy took a swig from her bottle. "Cal's bored, Francesca. You're not being a good hostess. Do you think he came all this way just to watch TV?"

"I'm not bored," said Calman. He kind of liked the idea of sitting quietly and watching TV.

"Calman, do you watch TV at home?" asked Francesca.

"Sometimes." As long as he finished his homework, his parents allowed him one hour an evening outside of unlimited news, nature shows, *Jeopardy!*, and anything on PBS. They had promised to let up on these kinds of rules after his bar mitzvah, but this one he'd gotten used to by now. "I like nature shows a lot."

"Yeah, well, we have our own nature show for you down-stairs, don't we, Francesca? Should we show Cal Dad's work-shop?"

"Okay. But can we play the pose game?"

"We can play the pose game, yes. Cal, follow us."

Calman followed Rizzy and Francesca down a creaking stairway to the windowless basement. It was dark and dank and smelled like wood varnish and something rotten.

"Have you seen Daddy's stuffed animals before?" asked Francesca.

"No," said Calman. *Did he want to?*

Rizzy turned on the light and Calman gasped. Atop wooden shelves were five mounted, upright mammals: three squirrels, a raccoon, and a black-and-white cat, all appearing as if they were looking right at him. And as if that weren't enough, in the middle of the room on a table was a rat skin pinned flat to a piece of heavy cardboard. A piece of index card was paper-clipped to each side of each of its ears.

"Are . . . are you sure we should be down here?" He couldn't look at the rat directly, not yet. Instead he looked around the workshop. There were two large buckets on the floor near the entranceway, and on the shelves with the animals was a mishmash of items: salt, baking soda, measuring spoons and cups, an electric shaver, yellow cornmeal, scalpels, cotton, wire, cardboard, moth flakes, Elmer's glue, and a framed license with Bob's name on it from the National Taxidermists Association propped up against the wall in the corner.

"Scared?" said Rizzy, menacingly.

"No, I . . ."

"It's okay if you're scared," said Francesca, climbing up on a stool. "I didn't like coming down here either, but now it's okay. You just have to think of the animals like they're on TV, like they're singing and dancing."

"Yeah," said Rizzy, "just like they're singing and dancing, only dead." She leaned over so her lips were close to the rat's face and pretended to adopt its voice. "Help, I need some *body*. Help, not just any *body*." She sang the Beatles tune in a falsetto with pursed lips, then drew away from the rat. "Get it? Body? Man, I'm funny sometimes."

Calman didn't really want to think about what happened to its body. "Why does it have clips on its ears?"

Rizzy put down her root beer bottle and picked up a scalpel off the shelf. "To stop the ears from curling as the skin dries," she said. "Bob says rats are easier to practice on than mice, they're bigger. He practices on road kill, too. See that raccoon? Road pizza."

"Rizzy, Mama doesn't like when you say 'road pizza.' "

"Well, *Mama* doesn't like when you're down in the work-shop. What do you say we don't tell her, okay?"

"Okay," said Francesca.

Rizzy continued talking to Calman. "Lily hates pretty much anything to do with Bob's hobby, which is why I'm in full sup-port of it. I mean, it makes sense he cuts up animals, he's a doc-tor, right?" She swished the scalpel in the air like a sword.

"One time this creepy old lady who walks the highway in the morning saw him picking up road pizza and asked him what he was doing. He told her, and the next day she brought him her dead cat, Mitzy. I swear Bob made it look like Mitzy came back to life. That's when he started doing people's pets." Rizzy looked down then.

Is she thinking of her dog? Calman wondered. He thought if he was going to say something, he should just say it now. "You know, I meant to tell you I'm sorry about Larry," he said, quietly.

She looked at him, looked away, took a moment, then talked as if she didn't hear what he'd said.

"Once the animal's skinned," she said, "you have to boil the bones. So you skin it, boil the bones, stick wire in the skull and string along the vertebrae, glue on other stuff, ribs, hind legs, tail, front legs, put the skin on, and *voilà*."

Calman looked up at the cat. He could have sworn he'd read a book once about a dead black cat coming back to life and haunting its owner. It had given him nightmares. "The eyes," he said, "how . . . how does he get the eyes to look so real?"

"They *are* real," said Rizzy in a low voice, leaning in. "They're looking at us from the underworld and they're—"

"No they're not, Rizzy," said Francesca, keeping the mood light. "They're glass. I know, Daddy told me. The eyelids are clay and the mouth is wax."

"Francesca," said Rizzy in her normal voice. "Where's your imagination?"

"Right here," said Francesca, tapping her finger to her head.

"Well, then, why don't you use it?"

"Because I don't want to now." She climbed off the stool and walked over to the raccoon to pet it gently. "I just imagine what I want to imagine, not what you tell me to imagine because you're just trying to scare us."

Rizzy laughed. "No fooling you, little girl. How'd you get to be so smart?"

"I just am," she sang.

Calman was glad Francesca was there. His eyes kept coming back to the rat. It was shocking at first, but now he was used to it and found it interesting, like nothing he'd seen before. Sort of like his experience meeting Rizzy.

"Know what this cornmeal is for?" Rizzy held the box in her hand. Calman shook his head. "To soak up all the blood."

That's just what he didn't need to hear. He began to feel a little woozy.

"Can't take the thought of blood?" She pressed the scalpel into the tip of her index finger until a drop of blood formed.

"Stop," said Calman, alarmed. "Don't do that. That's not funny."

"What?" said Rizzy, licking her finger clean. "It's only blood."

Calman remembered the events of that morning, about Rizzy yelling out that she was bleeding when they had her down on the ground, and about Sal's explanation of Rizzy just recently getting her period. She must be thinking a lot about that, he thought. He should get her to talk about it, that's what his therapist would say, but he didn't want to do that in this creepy room, and not in front of Francesca.

It seemed to Calman that Rizzy knew what he was thinking by the way she was looking at him. Her furrowed brow gave away her intention to say something confrontational, but thankfully Francesca interrupted.

"Strike a pose, Rizzy, strike a pose! Let's play!" she yelled.

Rizzy let the moment pass and indulged Francesca. "Okay, ready?" she said, moving to the other side of the room. "Cal, when I yell 'strike a pose,' you freeze in place and try to look like the animal you're closest to. Got it? Okay, move around, move around, that's it, now *strike a pose!*" At this she and Francesca stopped abruptly where they stood. Francesca, near the cat, curled her fingers and held them out like paws in mid-stride. She was trying not to giggle. Rizzy, by one of the squirrels, hugged the wall with her hands splayed as if she were climbing. Calman wasn't playing. "Cal, don't tell me you don't have any imagination, either."

"Rosalita?" Lily called out from upstairs. "Are you down in the basement? Francesca isn't there with you, is she?"

"Oh, no, I better go up," said Francesca. She left Calman and Rizzy and hopped up the steps.

Calman didn't yet feel comfortable being alone with Rizzy, and yet there they were.

Rizzy, not helping matters, approached Calman around the table and moved into his personal space. She put her face close to his, and he moved his head back a bit. She began twitching her nose like a mouse, sniffing him.

"What are you doing?"

She smiled wickedly. "I dare you to touch," she said.

She was so uncomfortably close to him. "Touch what?" he said. What did she mean? Touch her? Touch her where?

She backed off slowly, smiling, pointing to the table. "The rat," she said. "I dare you to touch the rat. What did you think I meant?"

Calman retreated to the door. The sights and smells and thoughts in the room were getting to him. He needed Pepto-Bismol. "I'm going to go upstairs now," he said, not waiting for a response.

This Little Light of Mine, I'm Gonna Let It Shine

Sunday morning had a scent and a texture all its own, like freshly bleached cotton sheets billowing on a clothesline under a warm sun. Calman was awake and wrapped around his pillow, smelling it, letting his mind soon wander off to hazy memories of early childhood, maybe even of infancy, when the greatest joy was the uninterrupted lingering between sleep and dreamy consciousness, and the waking into light and softness and safety.

Those were the mornings before the onset of Hebrew school, therapy sessions, and calisthenics designed for anxious adolescents, before his parents' early-morning complaints, muffled behind their bedroom door, of little time and little space, complaints that exploded into arguments at breakfast about little energy and lost patience.

This morning, though, felt like a true Sunday morning, for there was only the smell of sheets, the sound of small birds, and the movement of the gauzy curtains that swelled with the breeze above Calman's cot. He watched them rise and fall, and counted to himself: up, then down gently, and still. Ten. Up, a silent roll, down slowly, and still. Eleven. Sal's voice drifted in at thirteen.

"I wish it would cool off. We need some rain." Sal didn't jump out of bed, as he had done the day before. Instead, he stretched his limbs out catlike and yawned. "Have you been awake for a while?"

"A little while, I guess." Dust floated in the slanted sunbeams emanating from the window.

"You probably haven't been sleeping well, right? I can't sleep when I'm not in my own bed. Or when I'm alone." Sal glanced over at his brothers, balled in their beds against the far wall. "Guess I'm used to the sound of them."

Sal's voice purred. It was a tenor's lullaby, a whispered secret, an exhalation of well-being. Calman thought he'd like to get used to the sound of Sal. "Actually, I don't really sleep that well at home. I have insomnia."

"At home? Wow, that sucks. What do you do for it?"

"Sometimes I listen to relaxation tapes. One plays ocean sounds. Only, the week before I came here, my parents said I was listening to it, and when I fell asleep I started screaming that I was drowning, so they didn't think I should bring the tape with me on my trip. So I count things."

"You count sheep or something?"

"Well, no. But I could, I guess." There was silence again, and Calman thought of sheep. In his mind they were grazing in a meadow with cows and horses, too many and too unarranged to count, but somehow, at that moment, that felt okay.

"I wish we could sleep all day today."

"Yeah." Calman yawned a deep, long, arching yawn and let his eyes close. He was tired. And yet here was Sal, listening to him, asking questions of him, not laughing or criticizing him, and of all the times to feel sleepy. Calman fought to stick with the conversation. "My therapist says I can't sleep because I worry too much."

Sal didn't respond right away, which made Calman read something into his silence, a subtle change signifying curiosity perhaps, or, worse, estrangement.

"Why do you see a shrink?" asked Sal.

Calman was eight years old the first time he heard his therapist called a "shrink." He had had nightmares then, wondering what exactly his therapist was trying to shrink—his head, heart, hands, private parts? Three years later, he learned from one of his parents' dinner guests that that was silly, that his therapist wasn't exactly a shrink, and that the only thing his therapist was actually capable of shrinking, ha ha, was his ego.

"I don't know," he said. "I just always have, ever since I can remember. It's just something you do." Like brushing your teeth, thought Calman, or writing "Love, Calman" on birthday cards to relatives once or twice removed whose faces he couldn't recall.

The story of how his therapy visits began was one he'd heard many times, especially at his parents' catered dinner parties when he'd eavesdrop from around the bend of the dining room. When Calman was born, his parents had visited their local bank and launched two funds on his behalf—a college fund and a therapy fund—to which they still contributed a portion of their earnings. *What do you mean, a therapy fund?* he would hear one of his parents' friends ask. *It's the smartest thing a parent can do for a child,* one of them would say, eager for the opportunity to parade their ingenuity in front of their friends. *Let's face it, all families are dysfunctional, right?* Here his father would stand and wobble with his wineglass held high. *Our parents screwed us up, their parents screwed them up, and so on and so forth, that's the way it is. But we're the lucky ones. We live in a time of cognition. We can stop the cycle. Bridgette and I knew we had to do something when we became parents. We could do everything right and still our kid would be messed up. So we feel it's a parent's responsibility to head it off at the pass. Best thing we ever did for Calman, if you ask me, sending him to a therapist. I hate to think how much worse he'd be if we hadn't.* That was the line that Calman took away with him, back to bed and his nightmares. He could have been *worse*.

"Well, *I* don't see a therapist," said Sal.

"What?"

"I don't know anyone who sees a therapist, except you."

What Calman meant to say was that it was something *he* did. He had learned early and painfully that he was unlike other children in this regard. In a circle of third graders, Calman's teacher pointed out that one of the girls sitting across from him was inappropriately acting up. *Kara is angry, students,* she had said. *What do we do when we're angry? Calman?* Said Calman: *We tell our therapists.* There was laughter from the ones who knew what a therapist was, and odd, condescending looks from the ones who didn't know but would be told later at recess by the ones who did. Calman's teacher told his parents that he was a very honest boy, and that she was glad to learn that he was, well, you know . . . "special" . . . and that she wouldn't be so tough on him seeing as he was so fragile. Calman learned from that day on that when someone asked you what you did when you were angry, you told them take a deep breath and get over it.

"What do you talk about with your therapist?" asked Sal.

"Stuff. Anything."

"Can't you talk to your parents?"

"They don't really listen. They're caught up in their own issues."

"Issues," repeated Sal, first as if it were the oddest word in the English language, then again, softly, as if it were a mantra. He pulled an orange Nerf ball from behind his pillow and threw it up to the ceiling. Each time, it brushed against the wall soundlessly and landed in his outstretched hands in a mesmerizing arcing pattern. "Cal, are you messed up in the head?"

"Maybe I am," said Calman, watching the ball like an infant drawn to movement.

"So what do you worry about?"

"I don't know. If people like me or not."

Sal sat up at the edge of his bed, threw back his blanket, and scratched his groin. "I like you," he said, and then looked at the doorway. "And Rizzy likes you, right, Riz?" Sal walked over to Rizzy and faked a punch at her shoulder. Rizzy had a habit, Calman had noticed, of appearing in doorways. It was sort of creepy. She wasn't there, and then she was there, blocking his escape. Sometimes he had the feeling that she was like a key to his locked cage, only she was swinging outside the cage, just inches beyond reach, taunting him with the possibility of freedom—freedom from what, though, he didn't know.

"Who's asking?" said Rizzy.

"Calman," said Sal. "He's worried you don't like him."

Rizzy ignored Sal and looked at Calman in a way that made him run through the events of the last couple of days. Lately, he noticed her eyeing him curiously when she thought he wasn't looking, and not just the whole of him, but pieces of him, like his chest, hands, ears. This time, her gaze from the doorway slid up and down his extended body beneath the sheet, until his stare, like a magnet, forced her eyes to lock with his.

"I like raisins," she said. "I like raisins so much that one time I ate thirty-six little red boxes of raisins and my stomach cramped up so bad that Lily had to take me to the hospital where Bob was working so I would stop screaming and they could make me puke and empty out everything I had inside of me until I stank and drooled and dried up and when someone would ask me what went so wrong I'd say it all happened because I like raisins, maybe even love raisins."

Calman heard a slight squeak in his ears when he swallowed the saliva that was pooled at the base of his tongue. He thought his gulp might be visible in the way it extended his neck like a frog and slid down the back of his Adam's apple. How was it that one was able to hide fear, he wondered, when fear found a home in basic human functions like swallowing and blinking and breathing?

"That's a nice story, Riz. Real nice," said Sal. He walked over to where their three little brothers were beginning to wake up, turning and yawning and pulling at their covers. He poked at them with his elbows. "Get up, butt-heads, before your sister finishes turning into a hideous monster and eats you whole."

"Children," summoned Lily from downstairs in her singsong voice. "Get dressed now. It's time for church."

Rizzy spit out the side of her mouth and walked back to her room.

At ten o'clock, the Dickson children assembled in the living room for a thorough appearance check before church. Lily insisted on "inspecting the troops before battle," Sal told Calman, to ensure that no one would be caught with dirt under the fingernails, uncombed hair, unmatched socks, or untucked dress shirts.

"Brock, your shoelaces are untied. Fabio, fix your sleeves. We want to make a good impression, now. Quickly, quickly." Lily moved down the line of children and stopped in front of Rizzy. Calman saw her smile, at her daughter. It was a tentative, experimental smile, it seemed, but sincere and brave in its obvious attempt to make peace. "Rosalita, you look very pretty this morning," she said, reaching out to cup Rizzy's shoulder.

Rizzy hesitated for a moment, then pulled her shoulder away. "Don't you wish," she said, and rolled up her sleeves.

Lily gave Calman the choice of joining them or staying home with Tank, the local handyman, who had volunteered to miss church this Sunday to fix the leak under the kitchen sink. Tank's early-morning hammering was less offensive than his body odor, reminiscent of rotting roughage, and his tone-deaf rendition of Beethoven's Fifth Symphony, for which he used the syllable "bum" to sing each note. When Tank was introduced to Calman, he bellowed a "Hello there" as if Calman were far away across a great divide instead of standing right there next to him, and then smacked Calman in the shoulder, inadvertently sending his small body several feet across the floor and into a pile of recyclable soda cans.

Sal had described Tank to Calman when the two boys were getting dressed that morning. "I swear to you, it's true," Sal was saying. "He's got this weird speech thing that, once you hear it, you can't not hear it."

"What does he say?" asked Calman.

"He says, 'Roll it up a notch.' "

"What does that mean?"

"Nothing. That's just it. He says it as if he were saying 'um' or something. Wait, you'll see."

"Did anyone ever say anything to him?"

"I don't know. Not that I know. It's just him. I think he got screwed up in Vietnam or something."

This was the conversation Calman was remembering when Tank reached out his big paw, lifted him to his feet, and apologized.

"Jeez, you're a roll-it-up-a-notch little one, ain't ya? Gotta watch roll-it-up-a-notch guys like me, we don't know our own roll-it-up-a-notch strength. Sorry 'bout that, pal. No hard feelings? Hey, did you ever roll-it-up-a-notch hear the one about the one-legged prostitute who . . . "

"Um, excuse me," said Calman politely as he brushed himself off and backed out of the kitchen.

"Mrs. Dickson?" he said to Lily in the hallway.

"Yes, Calman," said Lily.

"Can I go to church with you?"

"Of course."

The Catholic church on the north side of Walla Walla was significantly smaller than Trinity Church in Copley Square at the center of Boston, the only other church Calman had been in. Since the doors of Trinity Church were usually open to tourists, Calman had followed a tour group in one day while his parents thought he was across the street at the Boston Public Library. The church seemed quieter than the library. He followed the tour guide down a side aisle and, because he was staring up at a stained glass window and not looking where he was going, he bumped into a woman standing by a tray of candles. Her eyes were closed and she held in her hand a long white candle with which she was about to light one of the candles on the tray. She turned around suddenly and clumsily lit his notebook on fire. Calman's scream echoed throughout the church, as did his stomping on his notebook to put out the fire. He complained of psychosomatic heat exhaustion for a week after that, though it was mid-November, and never went back for fear they would know for sure he was a Jew.

"Look, they're waiting in line to get in. You'd think they were giving away free booze or something," said Rizzy as they approached the front steps of the church. For the time being, Rizzy seemed to have forgotten any past weirdness between her and Calman. In fact, she appeared more tolerant than usual, even a bit possessive of this small boy from Boston walking close by and just a bit behind her. He had acquired a water mark in an unfortunate spot next to the zipper of his khaki pants that he was sure everyone noticed. He kept looking at himself down there and thought maybe if he widened his stride he could air out his pants and the mark would dry faster, only he caught a glimpse of himself in the church window, walking like a bowlegged cowboy with a Japanese fan on one hip and a bottle of Evian water on the other—both of which he carried in case he should feel faint again—and the thought occurred to him that he wasn't doing much to foster his desired anonymity.

"And who might you be?" said an important-looking man at the church's entrance.

"Mr. Johnson, meet Calman. He's my friend from Boston," said Rizzy.

She said friend, thought Calman. *Say it again.*

"He's our special guest," said Robert Dickson, shaking Mr. Johnson's hand. Rizzy's father was a commanding figure next to the average Walla Walla resident, and since he was one of the town's doctors and had such a casual and friendly way about him, he was well known and well liked and greeted jovially by many in the congregation.

"Welcome, Calman from Boston," said Mr. Johnson. "We're glad you could join us."

"I think I should tell you," said Calman to Rizzy, once they were inside, "I've never actually been to a church service."

"Piece a cake. You stand, you sit, you make faces at the choir," said Rizzy. "No sweat."

Though Lily said she preferred to sit up front, the rest of the Dicksons persuaded her to follow Simon and hide in back. Simon sat in a different seat every Sunday. He told Rizzy that God liked variety, but Rizzy told Calman that it really all depended on the first attractive woman he saw and where she sat.

"Look at Mrs. Callister this morning, Grandpa," said Rizzy,

pointing surreptitiously at a woman with a large bosom and red reading glasses.

"Good girl," he answered, and hurried toward a seat with a perfect angle for viewing.

Calman found the organ music rather somber for a place filled with floral patterns and aftershave. Though he hadn't planned it, he found himself sitting between Rizzy and Simon because of the nonchalant way they slid into the pews. "You'll have to do the poking, then, when he snores," said Rizzy, who had somehow got stuck next to Lily. The music stopped and the murmurs around the room subsided. A man behind a microphone bellowed something about the Father and the Son and everyone answered, "Amen." Then they all sat down.

"Ah, women," said Rizzy, who received a quick scowl from Lily.

After the first ten minutes, Rizzy became restless. She had such an excess of energy that fidgeting seemed to help very little. She cracked her knuckles and twirled her feet, and teased Calman by reaching behind him and tapping him on his far shoulder. The first time she did it, Calman had turned around and stared at the people behind him. He saw an older couple engrossed in their prayer books and assumed they weren't the type to tap him just for fun and then pretend they hadn't done it. He figured it was either Rizzy, who was in the midst of a staring contest with Sal, or Simon, who seemed to have found a woman worth staring at two rows back and across the middle aisle.

Calman was interested in seeing the women who intrigued

Simon McCory. He had an image in his mind of Simon hunched over his banjo in his white boxer shorts, a woman listening from behind, kicking her nyloned foot off the side of the unmade bed in his trailer. He remembered the redhead in a leopard-skin bikini on the January page of Simon's *Playboy* calendar and thought Simon might be partial to the voluptuous type with long hair. Or maybe he preferred a cute Southern belle with a cheery drawl and a gum-cracking smile, like one of the waitresses he saw at the diner.

"Hey, now there's a hot dame," Simon whispered to Calman with a manly grin. Simon nodded behind him and directed his eyes to the spot where Calman should look, but the congregation stood at that moment and he couldn't see. He waited for everyone to sit down again, and when they did, he took his opportunity. He turned slowly and stretched his neck, and then with a gasp he snapped it back in place. There, over shoulder pads and a woman with Baby Jesus earrings, was Mrs. Blenke in pink and pearls.

"Cal, sit," said Rizzy, pulling him down by the sleeve. "Jesus, it's not that hard, this church stuff."

Calman dropped into his seat.

"What do you think?" asked Simon, who was leaning over toward Calman and talking quietly out of the side of his mouth. "Quite a cutie, eh?"

Calman and Simon both turned back for another look. This time, Mrs. Blenke spotted Calman and waved at him with extreme vigor, which, Calman noticed, embarrassed not only him but also Oscar, who sat next to his mother and put his finger to his lips to quiet her.

"Hoo-wee. See that? She's all over me like a fly on sh—" said Simon, quickly remembering his surroundings. Obviously thinking she was waving at him, Simon turned to her and tipped his hat.

"You know her?" asked Rizzy, who had apparently seen the whole exchange and knew Mrs. Blenke had waved to Calman.

"Yeah. She's the one who drove me to your house," answered Calman, hoping Simon was too busy to eavesdrop on their conversation.

"How'd you meet her?"

"She sat next to me on the plane. She's from Seattle."

"Hush, children," said Lily, as the choir went on to something somber. Calman noticed how Lily sat very stiffly and moved her eyes about the congregation, examining dresses, hats, postures, sideburns, anything there was to look at. Bob Dickson, at the end of the aisle, on the other hand, stared straight ahead and looked like he was in deep thought.

"The lady who drove Calman from the airport is over there near old man Bueller," Rizzy explained to Lily.

"Well, actually her son gave me a ride," said Calman quietly, leaning over toward Lily. "He's the one with the beard, sitting next to her."

Rizzy and Lily turned to look. Mrs. Blenke was looking down at her hymnal, but Oscar saw Calman and nodded in his direction.

"Grandpa almost peed in his pants when he saw her," said Rizzy, imitating Simon with a lovesick grin.

"That's enough," whispered Lily. "Let's pay attention now. We'll see them after mass."

Rizzy and Calman turned again to look at Mrs. Blenke and Oscar, and noticed someone else smiling and waving over the toupees and dye jobs.

"Oh, gross," said Rizzy.

"What? What is it?" said Calman, above the thumping of his heart. He was somewhat excited to see Mrs. Blenke but wished their reunion could be under different circumstances. Perhaps in a field with no one around for miles, he thought, or on a plane heading back to Seattle.

"He's looking right at us."

"Who?" asked Calman, thinking she meant Oscar.

"Roland Gates," said Rizzy.

"Who's Roland Gates?" Calman realized he had spoken too loudly when Sal leaned over and entered the conversation.

"Where is he?" asked Sal. Rizzy pointed in his general direction. "I bet he'll ask you for a date," teased Sal. Rizzy looked remarkably like Lily when she scowled.

"Who's Roland Gates?" Calman asked again.

"He's the one I was telling you about. The one who has a crush on Rizzy," explained Sal.

"Children, calm down," interjected Lily. "It's almost over."

Rizzy and Calman turned to Simon and saw him wink at Mrs. Blenke. They turned to see what Mrs. Blenke would do and instead saw Roland Gates again. Roland, who had also seen Simon wink at Mrs. Blenke, tried winking at Rizzy by lifting his cheek and lowering his eyebrow. He got as far as a squint and gave up. Sal watched Roland, too, and started snickering and poking Rizzy in the thigh.

"Shut up," she said to Sal, while she reached over and put her arm around Calman.

"What are you doing?" asked Calman.

"Shh. Just play along. Pretend you're my boyfriend."

Calman peeked behind him. Roland stared at him with a look of confusion while Mrs. Blenke returned his glance with an oh-how-cute-you-have-a-girlfriend smile. Calman took out his Japanese fan and waved it in front of his face to dry the sweat near his temples.

"Will you put that away?" said Rizzy. "You look like the Queen of England. Relax."

"*Alvin!*" yelled Mrs. Blenke as she meandered through the crowd toward the Dicksons with Oscar in tow. The churchgoers funneling through the front doors scrutinized her. "What a surprise," she exclaimed as she reached down to touch his cheek. She wore a pink beaded hat.

"Hi," he said with a slight smile. He was glad to see her.

"I was so worried about you. We never even got a chance to say goodbye." Mrs. Blenke looked disapprovingly at Oscar.

"Mother, I told you I was sorry about that," he said. To Calman he added, "And I'll apologize to you, as well. She was really hoping she'd see you again." He held out his hand to Lily for a formal handshake. "Hi, I'm Oscar Blenke."

"Yes, of course," said Lily, slipping her hand into his grasp. "Calman told us all about you. Didn't you, dear?" She addressed Calman with only a slight turn of her chin, incurious if he was listening or even present at that moment.

"This is Lily," said Rizzy. "Her husband, Bob, stuffs dead things as a hobby."

"Rosalita!" cried Lily.

Rizzy said she often bragged of her father's skills as a taxidermist. She found that such information had a powerful effect on the younger kids.

Calman searched around for Mr. Dickson, but couldn't find him. He must have escaped outside.

"Well, now," said Mrs. Blenke with a brightness in her voice. "Who might you be?"

"Rizzy Dickson."

"Really? Alvin, is this your pen pal?"

Calman nodded, mentioning nothing about the mispronunciation of his name. "How peculiar," she said to Rizzy. "I was under the impression you were a boy."

Calman and Lily immediately turned toward Rizzy with the memory of her previous reaction to such a statement. They could tell a recurrence was imminent by the way Rizzy pursed her lips. Calman blushed and, in those brief few seconds, prayed to God that Rizzy would not indulge in a repeat performance. Lily, who possessed the acquired skill of someone who is used to defusing such episodes, was quick to interject. "Uh, and you are . . . ?"

"Eleanor Blenke." *Eleanor,* thought Calman. It had never occurred to him to ask about her first name. "Alvin and I were neighbors on the plane. We were wondering what happened to you at the airport." Mrs. Blenke eyed Lily accusingly.

Lily placed her hand in a V at the base of her neck. "Oh, we feel just awful about that. Our dog died that morning, and the children . . . Well, you can imagine the chaos. Robert was supposed to be there, but he just didn't realize the time."

"Mm," said Mrs. Blenke. She leaned in to Lily and said into her ear, "There's something hanging from your nose, dear," and then handed Lily a tissue from her purse.

Lily's hand flew up to cover her face. "Oh, excuse me," she said, and turned to the wall behind her. When she turned back around, it was clear that she had lost her chance at gentility, and out of habit began pouting and patting her updo and smoothing the material of her salmon-colored dress over her pear-shaped frame. The moment was not lost on Rizzy and Calman.

"That's one for *dear* Eleanor," whispered Rizzy to Calman.

Calman looked down at the floor and checked his own nose for boogers. He wanted to know if they had found his first-aid kit in the car and if he could get it back, but he didn't have the nerve to ask.

"Well, how do, ma'am?" said Simon, startling them from behind. Simon had been trying diligently to reach Mrs. Blenke since the service had ended. Calman had watched for a while and studied his talents at deflection. First, Simon had to get past Beatrice Lillicrop, who requested a donation from him for the Friends of the Petunias. The group, of which she was president, wished to save the delicate flowers from the rabbits, the dogs, and other munching animals, she explained. Simon dismissed her request with a dollar and, as he maneuvered away from the pews, bumped into eighty-year-old Horace Campbell, who asked if Simon would play the banjo at his twin brother's funeral.

"Horace," said Simon into his hearing aid, "your brother isn't dead yet."

"Yes, but he will be," said Horace. "Perhaps you could keep the month of September open with us in mind."

"Hello," Mrs. Blenke said to Simon.

"I'm Simon McCory. That's a mighty nice hat you have there. Always like women in hats. Makes a statement."

"Thank you. I noticed yours as well," said Mrs. Blenke, looking down at the hat dangling from Simon's fingertips. "I can't take mine off so easily. I'm afraid it's just about glued to my head with hair spray, if you know what I mean." Simon laughed.

Lily explained Simon's connection to her and Rizzy, and asked Oscar where he lived exactly and how long he'd been living in Walla Walla. Simon, eager to break into a private conversation with Mrs. Blenke, whispered more compliments to her about her attire.

"Psst," beckoned Sal to Rizzy and Calman, who had become increasingly bored with the conversation. "Come here," he whispered. Rizzy and Calman slipped behind Simon and followed Sal outside.

Sal had quickly disappeared after the service, he said, to avoid the inevitable cheek-pinching, hair-tousling, chin-grabbing attempts of Lily's baking group. There were thirteen of them. "A baker's dozen," Sal said, rolling his eyes. Once a week they met to try out a new recipe and a new pun for their bake-sale flyers. "Popover and check out the goods," said one. "Rise to the occasion," said another. They had names, too, for particular relatives of the group members. Lily's Rizzy was always a "tough cookie," but Sal was undoubtedly the "cutie-pie of Walla Walla." Calman wondered what pastry he'd be. "They're nuts," said Sal. "They're a bunch of fruitcakes," added Rizzy.

Calman winced at the heat and light of the sun as he left the church. He took refuge in the random dots of shade and the slight breeze that tickled the hair on his forearms. He fought the urge to reach again for the Japanese fan tucked into his back pocket.

Sal led Rizzy and Calman behind the church, where hopscotch boards drawn in neon chalk spotted one corner of the parking lot. Several kids were playing tag, and Calman immediately recognized the one who was it. It appeared as if Roland Gates, who looked older than the others, was repelling them in all directions.

"Hey," yelled Roland to Rizzy. He called a time-out, which prompted the players in the game to stop and walk toward him, as if drawn by some magnetic force.

"What do you want?" asked Rizzy as he sauntered over.

"Ooh, boys, set your phasers on stun. We don't want to kill this one yet, she may prove to be valuable."

"Oh, shove it, Gates, you Trek nerd."

Roland Gates looked like a figure in a Picasso painting Calman had seen in a museum. His eyes were close together, his nose was crooked, his hair was gelled and spiked in various directions, and he had buttoned his shirt so that the bottom corners were asymmetrical.

"Aw, Riz," said Roland with a patronizing shove, "you're looking so girly in that dress a yours."

Calman looked around for Sal, who had conveniently left them alone to confront "Captain Jerk," as Rizzy called him. Calman saw Rizzy's fingers curl over her palms. He sensed an oncoming asthma attack.

"Like you know anything about girls, you fat lard," she said.

"Fat lard? Why you bringing your mother into this?"

Rizzy tightened her eyes and eyebrows and extended her lower lip. "Don't you ever talk about my mother that way, you got that? She's tougher and stronger than you'll ever be, trust me on that. She can kick your idiot ass into tomorrow."

The sincerity and seething control with which Rizzy spoke caught Calman by surprise. It was the first time he had ever heard her say something positive about her mom. Would he do the same if it was his mom? he wondered.

Roland kicked a hump of gravel that created a small dust

cloud by his feet. "Y'know, Riz, you're all talk, did anybody ever tell you that?"

"What's that supposed to mean?"

"What do you *think* it means?" Rizzy's and Roland's noses were now inches apart. Rizzy's brown hair fell behind her shoulders as she folded her arms against her torso and cocked her chin.

Roland, for the first time, noticed Calman standing nearby and recognized him from the church service.

"Who are you?" he yelled at Calman with a threatening, condescending full-body scan. Calman suddenly felt naked and cold. He counted to ten to slow his breathing.

"Calman Pulowitz," he said timidly. Rizzy looked at Calman. Calman stared at the ground. It looked hot and hard and generally uninviting with its tiny pebbles that would make indentations in his skin and find their way into his shoes and underwear.

"What kind of name is Calman Pulowitz?"

"It's Jewish," he said. He heard nervous laughter from the few children standing around them. He smiled at Roland in a way he hoped would be perceived as a white flag.

"Jewish?" said Roland.

Given his knack for poor timing and inappropriate gut reactions, Calman, at that moment, began to laugh. He didn't know why he was laughing, or why Rizzy, too, had started laughing. He could feel its effect on Roland, but he couldn't stop. He had as little control over his laughter as he did over hiccups or sneezes, despite his sense of impending doom. His eyes began to tear. He tilted his glasses up and sopped up the moisture with his sleeve.

"Poor baby, did I make you cry?" Roland tossed a monosyllabic laugh over his shoulder at the other boys.

In that moment, Calman made eye contact with one of those other boys, his doppelgänger, standing back, pushing up the nosepiece of his glasses, looking genuinely nervous and sympathetic and relieved, perhaps, that the brunt of Roland's Level Ten intimidation was not focused on him. In that fleeting glance, Calman understood that this boy, this follower of boys, was a body for a bully's army, that armies were made of many followers like them and that—when you took into consideration the East Coast, the West Coast, the whole country, the whole world even—maybe he wasn't really as alone as he thought he was.

"What a wuss," said Roland. "And you think you're man enough for Rizzy, you little sissy?"

Roland had little time to look pompous. In one fluid motion, Rizzy twisted her torso, swung her fist out with the force of uncanny machismo, and punched Roland in the face. He stumbled backward and held his cheek in disbelief, moving his jaw from side to side to assess the damage. Then he lunged at Rizzy, only Calman was quicker. Not knowing exactly what to do, Calman whipped out his Evian water bottle like a gun and squirted Roland in the eyes. This stopped Roland momentarily.

"What the . . ." slurred Roland as he wiped his face with the inside of his elbow and redirected his attack. This time he lunged at Calman, but Calman was quick again. He moved slightly to the left and stuck out his foot, tripping Roland in mid-lunge. Roland lost his balance, fell sideways, and rolled several feet away onto the shoes of old blind Mrs. Lickshore, who'd wandered around to the back of the church.

"*Ah.* Get off. *Off,* you perverted mutt!" she yelled, assuming the figure hanging on to her thick ankles was a lascivious Chihuahua that had run over to get a piece of the action. She hit Roland Gates repeatedly with her cane until he rolled out of her reach.

"Let's get out of here," said Rizzy to Calman. They ran back toward the front of the church and bumped into Oscar, Mrs. Blenke, and the whole Dickson clan on their way out.

"Oh, Calman, we were looking for you," said Lily. "Oscar and Eleanor will be joining us for dinner next Thursday. Isn't that nice?" Lily and Simon both looked as if they had won a lottery. "That will be Calman's last night with us," she said to Eleanor. "We'll give him a proper send-off."

"We'll see you then," said Mrs. Blenke to Calman, as everyone said their goodbyes. Calman's heart was racing.

"Rosalita, where did you run off to?" asked Lily as the Dicksons headed for home. The church was only three blocks away, making it a convenient jaunt to confession.

"Nowhere. We just had to take care of something," she said, and looked at Sal. Sal smiled and hid behind Bob. A tractor vibrated to their left as they rounded the bend toward the house. Bob and Lily waved to its tired, sweaty driver.

Rizzy and Calman walked ahead of the rest, until Calman broke off into a fast sprint. He felt the need to run, to race down the street and up a tree and yell something triumphant at the sky just to keep his heart beating the way it was, making it beat even faster to see how fast it would go, how strong and mighty he could be, how much of his physical self he could release from the confines of his lifelong emotional entrapments. Rizzy caught up to him at the house. She found him standing on a tree stump, squirting water from his Evian bottle high into the air and letting it splash onto his upturned forehead. Somewhere, so faintly as to be almost too far away, his mother's voice was telling him to stop wasting good water, and his therapist was asking why he had tripped that boy, why he was acting so immaturely. But all Calman could think of at the moment was that he had exerted himself—not the mental or emotional kind of exertion he was used to that left him exhausted and curled in a fetal position, but a new Herculean kind of exertion—and it made him feel like a giant among men.

"Damn," said Rizzy, out of breath after their run. "You're fast. I didn't think you had it in you." She walked in a circle around the stump where he stood. For a moment he was aware that she was looking up at him—admiringly, he imagined, the way a damsel just saved from some peril might look upon Superman in his fists-on-hips, legs-apart, cape-flowing stance. Calman smiled broadly and inhaled air so fresh his lungs expanded twice as much as ever before. If this was a cartoon, he'd unzip his nerd exterior and toss it aside like a rubber suit. Rays of sunshine would spring from his palms and a chorus of trumpets would burst into chords of glory.

"Your Excellency . . . Sir . . . My Lord . . . When you're done exulting to the heavens, would you do me the honor of coming down from there and sitting your skinny ass on the grass?" Rizzy lay on the ground, her dress already splotched with dirt stains.

Calman stepped down and sat next to her. They shared a silence of funny afterthoughts.

"I've never won a fight before," said Calman.

"Yeah? Well, that wasn't exactly winning, but it was pretty cool. We make a good team."

Calman lay down and looked up at the clouds. There were two of them, moving slowly side by side. Though they were shaped differently, they were in perfect sync, periodically intermingling their edges of white smoke in a comfortable airy embrace. In a sudden palpable, visceral way he felt connected to Rizzy. They were a team, a twosome of equal but separate parts moving through the world in search of the whole.

"High five," said Rizzy. Rizzy and Calman smacked hands in the air, marking a moment Calman would not soon forget.

The next day there came a letter from his mother.

The Water Is Wide, I Cannot Get O'er

By the next morning, Calman was no longer a mighty giant of a man. Bad things, his grandmother often repeated like a mantra, came in threes, and Monday—what turned out to be a rather ordinary day in the life of the original Calman Pulowitz—supported her statement.

First came the FedEx delivery man, who destroyed Calman's triumph with a missive from his mother. Each day she called on her cell phone, but the few conversations they had when he was there to receive the calls were always quick—*You okay, darling? I'm fine, Mom. What have you been doing? Nothing. I can't hear you, honey. I said nothing, Mom. You're breaking up, Calman, Mommy loves you.* She might have e-mailed, too, but Calman didn't want to bother anyone by using the computer in the study. Her letter, though, was no surprise, as she had said if he could "get into this letter-writing thing," so could she.

Inside the express package was a mauve envelope. Enclosed in the envelope was a Barney boo-boo strip and his horoscope—or horrorscope, as he got used to calling it—cut from some women's magazine. "Virgo," it read:

> Pump up the volume, turn on the charm;
> Kisses on these Gemini nights are sure to be five-alarm.
> Be sassy, be sweet, give in to impulses and feel the heat.
> There'll be some bloating mid-month, but all will clear
> When the planets align and July is near.
> Sleep tight, say "No" to stress;
> Open your heart and help others confess.
> Stay calm, keep your nervous tendencies at bay,
> And others will listen to what you have to say.

His mother had double-underlined the last two lines, and written above them, "Words to the wise." On the outside of the letter, which was folded neatly in thirds, was "More words to the wise," topped off with a misshapen smiley face with Marge Simpson hair and drop earrings.

> Calman, my sweet:
> How are you, darling? Did you survive the trip without an attack? Are you feeling okay, my little Fruity Pebbles?

You left for Washington this morning without your little stuffed penguin. Did you realize you forgot it? This could be a big step for you, doll. It might be that you subconsciously wanted to leave it behind. Maybe you felt ready to experience the next stage of life on your own. Each little step is a triumph, sweetheart.

Well, we're on our way to the Florida Keys. I'm sure we forgot something—you know how that goes. Oh, but not our suntan lotion, of course. God forbid. Your father brought two tons of full-strength sunblock, as if the ozone layer has already given up on the earth's tourist spots. Well, I'm going to get savagely brown while I still can. But you be careful, Calman. You're in dry heat, and you have very sensitive skin like your father. Stay in the shade, pumpkin.

I can't wait to get out to the beach. Daddy wants to windsurf, but I keep reminding him of his bad knees. He can't seem to accept that he's getting older. We all get older, Calman. Remember that. Anyway, I'm sure we'll have some wonderful pictures—you know what a ham I can be. Oops, off for now. We're about to land to catch our connecting flight. More later.

Back again. It's been a long day so far. Too long and Mommy's tired. I had to wait until your father fell asleep to catch up on some of my women's magazines. He said the odor of perfume suffocated him every time I flipped a page. I think he's exhibiting anxiety about being away from home.

Oh, Calman, your father and I . . . [and here she crossed this out and began again.] *Sweetheart, let's all just have a*

wonderful vacation and miss each other and talk when we get back, okay?

Poodle, are you getting enough protein? Make sure you're eating right and watching your cholesterol, darling. It's meat country out there—rural townspeople don't pay much attention to their cholesterol. You have enough vitamins to last you the trip, don't you?

Now, I know there won't be enough time to send a letter back to us, but you can write it and keep it and give it to us at home, okay? I'll do that, too, honey. It'll be fun.

Calman, take care of yourself. You're a big boy now. Your father and I miss and love you very much.

> *Au revoir, peaches.*
> *—Mom*

Calman's mother had a way of making him feel like a balloon at a porcupine convention. For moments at a time during his stay in Walla Walla, he had forgotten about her, but those moments passed quickly and left him drenched in his own meekness. It didn't matter that she was thousands of miles away. She was there, as real as ever, through manicured fingers to fancy pen, pen to scented paper, paper to his stubby paws; she was as tangible, as unignorable as a straitjacket. Surely, he thought, no one ever called James Bond "peaches." And what did she mean by they had to talk when they got back? Her crossed-out words screamed out like an explosion. Talk about what? What was wrong? He didn't want to think about it.

It was the letter that first brought him back to his familiar world, not to be outdone by a most mortifying game of truth or dare, followed by a deflating discovery in Rizzy's room.

While Calman read his letter, Rizzy and her siblings had convened in the yard for some afternoon mischief. They found Calman in a heap by the tree stump, flimsy-limbed and acquiescent.

When it was his turn to tell the truth or be dared, he picked the truth. Their game-truths were about peeing in the shower and pooping in the pool and, although his stark and dark truths rattled his skull like prisoners behind bars and had no business on the outside, particularly not to be broadcast to a pack of child voyeurs, speaking the truth seemed an easier humiliation than actually *doing* something.

But Rizzy wouldn't have it. "Forget it. We've had too many truths in a row. You have to do a dare."

"No, I don't," said Calman in a voice whinier than he had intended. "I thought I got to choose."

"Well, sometimes you don't."

"Forget it, then. I'm not playing."

"God, you're such a sissy," she hissed. "You're such a *girl*."

She knew just how to get to him. That was dare enough. "Fine. I'll do a dare if you do a truth and I get to ask the question." Not surprisingly, Rizzy always picked a dare and avoided the truths.

"This isn't a negotiation here. I already had my turn."

Calman challenged her with his eyes and then began walking away. "Then I'm not playing."

"Okay," she called after him. He stopped. "But you first."

The pressure was on for a very creative, highly educational dare, said Rizzy, that could prove, once and for all that, generally speaking, drool has a distinct smell.

"No, it doesn't," said Sal. "It smells like what you just ate. You don't know what you're talking about."

"Drool doesn't smell. That's stupid," said one of the little brothers.

"I swear it does," declared Rizzy. "Once it slides out of your mouth, it has its own smell."

That was the premise for Calman's research in droolenetics, research that soon had him inches from Simon's snoring mouth, ready to scrape—delicately, of course, so as not to wake him—droplets of spittle from Simon's chin into a glass for proper sniffing. The logic behind capturing the excretion of Rizzy's grandfather versus that of someone in the game was very complex and convoluted and had something to do with the fact that Simon was asleep, making the specimen true drool instead of mere saliva. Or something like that. Calman had dispensed with rules and logic in games with the Dicksons.

Two clouds had divided and multiplied like cells, crowding out the sun and turning the sky into an old black-and-white movie. From some distant radio, a sports announcer exclaimed over whistles and commotion. Every now and again, the air smelled of car wax. Calman tried unsuccessfully to concentrate on these sensory details to stop his hands from sweating. He approached Simon lying in a lounge chair by his trailer. Rizzy coaxed him on. He drew in close. The hairs of Simon's bushy salt-and-pepper beard were thick and curved at the ends in random directions. His eyeballs rolled beneath his eyelids, his nostrils flared slightly, honking in a steady rhythm. His skin sported wrinkles like runoffs from a stream, and his mouth, partially hidden in the shade of his beard, whispered and sighed in Calman's ear. If only Calman could be assured that Simon would stay asleep, he would study this man's face for answers to age-old questions. He would stay close to Simon's mouth to feel his breath on his own face, he might even reach out and touch his beard or the worry lines on his forehead. He might blow into his ear to see him flinch, or tickle his chin to see the teeth of his smile.

"Oh . . ." said Simon, soft and breathy with sleep. "Oh, Eleanor . . ."

Calman jumped back and flung the glass behind him. It hit the pavement, crashed, and woke Simon from soporific bliss. Calman's audience was in stitches.

"That was awesome," said Rizzy through her laughter. "Were you kissing him?"

"Calman ki-issed Grandpa. Calman ki-issed Grandpa," sang Francesca.

"No," said Calman. "I was . . . you were . . ." He looked at Simon. "It was a dare."

Simon rubbed the sleep from his face and chuckled softly.

"Kissed me, did ya? Hell, I thought you were Eleanor. Hoo-wee. Lucky I didn't kiss you back, eh?"

Calman counted in his head—one, two, three—to curb his nausea, while his playmates laughed themselves silly. How was it that he was able to block everyone out then and not now? Calman ran up to Sal's room and from a newly purchased bottle took a large swig of Pepto-Bismol, the drink of the emasculated, the drink of dolls and darlings and sweethearts. Why couldn't he be normal, like other kids? This was the second time since he'd been there that he had been mistaken for a female. Calman slumped to the floor and hung his head in defeat. At his bar mitzvah they said he was a man now. A man. They meant that he was a man now, not a boy, but why did it feel like they meant he was ready to be male now, not female?

When it became apparent that the Dickson children were going to let him be, Calman took a sheet of paper from his knapsack and began a response to his mother's letter. "Dear Mom," he wrote and then stared at the blank page until his eyes blurred. He pulled it close to his face and the whiteness expanded like a sandstorm in a vast desert where he knew the nearest shelter was not truth but platitudes. He tried hard, as he had tried over the last several years, to keep the tracks separate between what he wanted to say and what he knew he should say. He knew how to avoid collisions. After all, what could his parents really do from thousands of miles away? He wrote, and thought, and daydreamed, and wrote:

Hi from Walla Walla. I've only been here for three days, but so far it's okay. It's really hot.

I found out Rizzy is a girl. You probably know that by now from talking to Mrs. Dickson. I also found out that her dog (Larry) died the day I got here. Her family seems nice. She has four brothers and a sister, who all share rooms. Rizzy's brother Sal showed me how he can go from the top of his bed to his sister's bed next door without ever touching the floor. I haven't tried it yet.

I sleep in Sal's room, but I can hear Rizzy in the next room through the wall. She talks in her sleep. Last night she screamed in the middle of the night and woke us all up, but she said it wasn't her. We both have problems sleeping, I guess, but at least I know I do and I try to count things. Rizzy won't even admit it. Though, even if it's quiet at night, I stay awake sometimes because there aren't any streetlights outside and there's no traffic.

Rizzy's father is really tall, and her grandfather laughs a lot. He sleeps out in a trailer. Rizzy said her family kicked him out of the house because he sheds all over the furniture. That's why he's balding on top. She said they will let him back in when he has no more hair. I never met Larry, but the hair all over the house that Rizzy showed me and told me was her grandfather's sure looks like dog hair to me. I think she doesn't tell the truth all the time.

I met a nice lady on the plane from Seattle. She talked a lot, but I didn't care. It took my mind off flying. Her son gave me a

*ride to Rizzy's house from the airport. Rizzy was busy with
Larry's funeral.*

*I know you told me to write, but I don't know what else to
tell you. I hope you're having a fun vacation. I miss you.*

Your only son, Calman

He reread what he had written. Bland stuff, really. He knew
that. He thought about asking what it was she wanted to talk
about, but then didn't see the point. Maybe if he ignored that
part of her letter it would go away. Besides, no one wanted to
read his letters anyway, so why bother making an effort? Rizzy,
well, she probably had to, and she made a game out of looking for something to argue with or poke fun at. Certainly his
grandmother never read his letters. She was thrilled to get
them, but their contents might just as well have been a laundry
list of activities that she could use as evidence in a fight with his
mother over how much she'd missed of his growth during the
periods when his mother so inconsiderately kept them apart.
Even on the phone his grandmother never really seemed to
want to talk to him. She had a standard dismissive response to
anything he said that slammed the conversation into a brick
wall in about three minutes.

"I got an A on my vocabulary quiz, Grandma."

"Oh, very nice. You'll be a famous doctor or lawyer someday. So vat else?"

"Um, I don't know. Mom bought me undershirts yesterday.
Macy's was having a sale."

"White?"

"Yeah."

"Goot. Your shirts are too thin. Tell your mother to buy you new shirts. So vat else?"

Mom and Dad abandoned me in a field of onions.

Very nice. So vat else?

"Nothing else," he would say eventually, and she would tell him he was a good boy and that would end it. Calman's father would joke that she'd rush to her other grandmother friends and one-up them with news that her grandson had called. She'd get two points in the My Family Cares game for the call, and one point for each fact about his life she could brag about. No doubt she was losing the game, thought Calman. It ran in the family.

He folded his letter and searched for an envelope, and when he couldn't find one, he walked quietly toward Rizzy's room to take one from her desk, as he had remembered seeing some there before. Almost everyone was outside, so it was quiet upstairs, except for the soft noises coming from the bathroom of the master bedroom—little splashes of water, bumps against porcelain, a whistled tune. Lily was taking a bath. Calman could see a reflection in a mirror of the splayed and sudsy toes of her right foot hanging over the side of the tub. Why didn't she close the bathroom door, he wondered, or even her bedroom door? Maybe she wanted to keep an ear open to what was going on with her children. In front of the mirror near the bedroom door was her dresser, and atop her dresser Calman saw a picture of a smiling Dr. Dickson holding a big fish.

Rizzy's dad was an enigma to Calman. Like a family pet, he seemed pleasant and loyal and comforting, but also impenetrable when it came to figuring out what he was thinking about. He did, after all, have a strange hobby of stuffing dead animals. What kind of a person would like doing that? Bob Dickson seemed content to do his own thing until Rizzy's mom needed him, for she clearly ran the show. That was the way it was in his family, too, thought Calman. His dad was usually quiet and eccentric, a finicky vegetarian always with his nose in a book, except lately he'd been exceptionally vocal in response to Calman's mother's demands instead of being amused or ignoring her. It occurred to Calman that much of the communication he'd been having with his father lately was through his mother. *Tell Dad,* he'd say to his mom. *Your dad says . . . ,* she would say as often.

Calman decided to call his father. He found his dad's personal cell phone number in his bag and called on the phone that sat on a small table in the hallway. "Dad," he said, surprised when he heard his dad's hello.

"Calman? Is that you? Are you all right? Is anything wrong?"

"I'm fine. I'm glad you answered. I thought I'd just call and say hi."

"Oh." Calman heard voices in the background and a wide-open, windy sound that he thought might be the ocean. "Well, that's nice of you, son. It's good to hear from you. Your mother—"

"Dad," said Calman quickly. He didn't want to talk to his mother just now. "Rizzy's a girl. Did Mom tell you?"

He thought he heard his dad chuckle. "Yes, yes, she did say something about that after she talked to Mrs. Dickson the first time after we arrived. Calman, I'm shocked. I just assumed . . . Well, I mean, I talked to Mr. Dickson myself and it never occurred to me to, well, you know. Calman, how are you reacting to this? All that time you were writing to a girl! Did she conceal her gender on purpose, do you think?"

"I think she did, yeah. But it's okay. She was kind of hard to talk to at first, but I think she's starting to get used to me."

Yes, another gin and tonic please, thank you, said his father in a muffled voice, and then to Calman: "Is she pretty?"

Calman wasn't prepared for this question. He blushed. "I guess, I mean, I don't know. Dad," he said quickly to change the subject, "are you having a good time?"

There was a pause. "Why, yes, Calman. It's very nice here. The weather is beautiful." He paused again. "It's nice to get away from home every once in a while—lets a man ponder. Don't you think that's true, Calman?"

"I don't know. Maybe."

He heard his father say to someone else that he'd be right there. "Calman, your mother is getting a facial. Do you want me to have her call you back when she gets done?"

"No, that's okay."

"All right, then, we'll talk again soon. I'm glad you called. Call me anytime. I love you, son."

But what are you pondering? Calman wanted to ask. *Can we do more things together when we get home?* "I love you, too, Dad," he said, and hung up. He left his hand on the phone for a moment. It felt good to hear his dad's voice, but for some reason he felt a little empty and disappointed.

Still thinking of what to make of his conversation with his dad, Calman walked away from Lily's room, which smelled sweet like lilacs, and entered Rizzy's room to search for an envelope.

Her desk was a mess. There were pens and stickers and Tootsie Rolls and ribbons. Precariously placed on the edges were cups of small things like paper clips and pennies, an open bottle of perfume, and a half-melted candle, part of which had already spilled onto the floor. The centerpiece was an old typewriter, the very same one Calman heard clacking away whenever Rizzy was in her room, and next to the typewriter was some sort of manuscript turned facedown. All week Calman had wondered what Rizzy was typing. She typed quickly, that was for sure. Maybe she had several pen pals. Maybe they came all year round in one-week intervals. Curious, he looked behind him, then turned over and read the top few pages of the manuscript.

It was shocking. At the top of the first page in bold letters it read: "Hot Lava Love." The text underneath seemed to be the start of a racy romance novel in a place called Red River Valley about a woman named Victoria Veronique Vesuvius. Victoria had a crush on Ramon but was jealous of Genevieve and was in bed with bad, mad Bradford and *oh my God*, the things they were doing under canopied lace! Calman was blushing and breathing heavily.

"Hey, what are you doing?" yelled Rizzy, making one of her sudden doorway appearances. She rushed to her desk and grabbed the pages from Calman's shaking hand.

"Sorry," said Calman. "I was looking for an envelope and, well, I always hear you typing. I mean, I was curious . . ."

"Well, it's none of your business."

"Sorry." He was a slow reader and was swept into the story, so that while his visit to Red River Valley was only minutes in real time, it was seemingly infinite in mind-time.

Rizzy circled him, studied him up and down in tense minutes of silence, then sat on the bed. "So what do you think of it?"

"I don't know. What is it? Did you write it?"

"Hell, yeah. Good stuff, huh? Hey, what's that in your hand? You wrote something, too?"

The letters to and from his mother now hung limply from his grip.

"I got a letter from my mother, so I wrote her back."

"Can I read them?"

"No."

"Too late." Rizzy snatched the letters from his hand and moved away from him so he couldn't snatch them back.

"Everything all right in here?" said Lily, poking her head in. Fresh from her bath, she smelled like a garden.

"Fine," said Rizzy. Lily went downstairs.

Rizzy sat on her bed and read the letter from his mother aloud. " 'Your little stuffed penguin'? 'Peaches'? What are you, three years old?"

Calman felt weak. He stared at his sneakers.

"Does she really talk like this?"

"Sometimes, I guess."

"Is your dad like this, too?"

"Like what?"

"Like all foofy-poo and suffocating."

"I don't know." He thought of his brief conversation with his dad. "He's not as good a communicator as my mother is."

"Communicator? What, is he an android? Your brain's polluted with I don't know what. No wonder you're such a nerd. What do you think they want to talk to you about? They're probably—" she said and stopped. She must have seen the hurt in Calman's eyes, for he felt on the verge of crying. "It's probably nothing. Never mind," she said quietly. "And sorry, I didn't mean what I said. You're not a nerd. I'm just kidding."

Calman turned away and looked out the window.

"Hey," she said, "you want to know more about my book? I'll tell you if you promise you can keep a secret." She tapped the manuscript on her desk.

For the sake of saving face, Calman buried his hurt and

found the strength in a deep breath to leave it behind for the time being. "It's a book?" he said.

"Well, it's a chapter of a book. Do you promise?"

"I promise."

"Follow me."

Calman stood and collected himself, then followed Rizzy down to the kitchen, where Lily sat in a corner absorbed in a worn paperback. The other Dickson children were still playing outside.

"Lily," Rizzy barked, startling her the way she had startled Calman. Lily cleared her throat and hid her book on her lap under the table. "What are you reading?"

"Nothing of interest, dear. How are you children getting along?" She patted her disheveled updo.

"I think the mail just came," said Rizzy.

"Oh!" replied Lily, as if Rizzy had just announced the arrival of a Hollywood star. "Well, I'll go check the mailbox." Lily hurried out. The soles of her feet made a slapping sound against her mules as she moved down the hallway.

Rizzy peeked into the hall to make sure Lily was out of earshot, then opened a cabinet next to the refrigerator with a key she pulled from a pocket in her shorts. A paperback fell to the floor, shoved out by four shelves jam-packed with similarly worn, pastel-colored romance books.

"You wrote all these?"

"Yeah, Einstein. I've been writing them since I was three years old."

"Right," said Calman sheepishly. "Are they yours?"

"No . . . They're Lily's. She's so hooked on these things she's like a drug addict. She doesn't know it, but I've read them all. I stole her key once and made a copy of it."

Calman picked up the book from the floor and flipped through its pages. On the cover was a young, dark, bare-chested man astride a stallion, the wind in his flowing brown hair and a fiery sunset behind him. Would Rizzy notice if he snuck the book under his shirt? Too big a risk, he thought, and stuffed it back on the shelf. "Why does she keep them locked up?"

"She's afraid they'll corrupt our young minds. She likes to keep this her own little escape world. She thinks she's so mannered and prissy, but she doesn't fool anyone, at least she doesn't fool me."

"What are you doing?" yelled Lily, suddenly upon them in her furry high-heeled mules. "Close that immediately! How dare you!" She shoved Rizzy aside and slammed the cabinet door shut, Mr. Hyde–like. "How did you get in there?" She squeezed Rizzy's wrist and fumed through her nostrils. Her elbows—little pink dimples in folds of white flabby skin—were inches from Calman's nose. "These are mine. They are *not* yours. See that lock? That means they are off-limits, do you understand me?"

"Ow, you're hurting me."

"Do you understand?"

"What's the big deal? We were just—"

"You listen to me, Rosalita—"

"That's not my name."

"That has been your name since birth, and I don't care if you don't like it. You hear me? I'm your mother—"

"Are not."

"Oh, for God's sake, I'm sick of your antics. I'm sick of your rebelliousness. I'm sick of you always trying to undermine me. You don't like it here? You don't like me? Too bad. We're stuck with each other. The Lord's nasty joke, maybe, but that's the way it is. We all have to accept the life we've been given—"

"Oh, like you have?" screamed Rizzy, wrenching her arm out of Lily's grasp. "Is that why you bury your brain in these books?"

Lily smacked Rizzy across the face.

"Yeah, hit me!" screamed Rizzy. "Did that feel good? You can't stand the sight of me and I'm not even in a wheelchair!"

Calman didn't understand. What did a wheelchair have to do with anything?

Lily gasped. Her eyes filled with tears. "That's enough," she whispered. She tucked loosened bobby pins back into her lop-sided French roll, and sighed. "You will not—I repeat, *not*—open this cabinet again, is that clear?"

Rizzy rolled her eyes and opened the door to the backyard.

"Answer me," said Lily.

"Whatever," said Rizzy. "C'mon, Cal, let's get out of here."

Calman and Rizzy hopped on bicycles for a long ride around town and eventually to the state penitentiary. Calman rode Sal's bike, since Rizzy had demanded that Sal stay home. Calman was *her* friend, she pointed out, not his. Sal said he was busy anyway, that he had promised Francesca he'd go running with her through the sprinklers, and that was fine with him.

The two of them rode for what seemed to Calman like hours: past endless fields of windblown wheat and ranch-style houses with barking dogs and fenced-in horses. They passed pea fields, too, and strawberry fields, and pickers bent over onion fields, filling big sacks. A few times Calman had lost sight of Rizzy. He would then stop and sit down on the side of the road, feeling like he was going to throw up his set of internal organs. His heart and lungs hurt, and it was just too hot to push it.

At the edge of the penitentiary grounds, Rizzy and Calman dropped their bikes and bodies down on a patch of shaded grass. They were near the wardens' houses, and the area looked like a park or a college campus. The grass was trimmed, flowers were in bloom, and all Calman could hear was the birds and the laughing of nearby guards.

"This is the prison?" asked Calman.

"Yeah, over there. You'd think it was like a country club in there, though it gets creepier around back near the dairy farm. You can see the lookout tower and huge brick walls."

Calman leaned up on his elbows. There was something unsettling about the whole place. "Do you come here a lot?"

"I guess," said Rizzy. "I tried to get in once. Told them my father was in there and I had to see him."

"What'd they say?"

"They didn't buy it. Sent me home with a stupid lollipop like I'd been to the dentist. Then they called Lily. Man, she was madder than hell. Said they should have kept me locked up with the rest of those crazies." Calman turned away from the guards and looked at Rizzy, who was staring off into the distance at a car on the road. Rizzy seemed softer, less menacing for some reason than when he had first met her. She had scabs all down her long legs, but her skin was still smooth, and her shoulder-length brown hair sparkled red in the bright sun. She wore it in two braids, with loose strands that she kept tucking behind her multi-pierced ears. Her face, which Calman had never really stared at before, was filled with soft curves around her lips, over her cheekbones, and down the bridge of her nose. She had a birthmark on her neck shaped like a three-quarter moon.

"What are you looking at?" Rizzy snapped.

"Nothing." Calman's breathing had finally slowed nearer to its normal pace, but he wasn't yet ready to get up. He felt strange, as if he was both tired from the ride and energetic from knowing that he had done it. They sat for a time in silence, watching two squirrels stop and run between two oak trees. A yellow butterfly dipped between them and flapped around erratically, then flitted up to the sky.

"Let's say," said Rizzy, now lying on her stomach and pulling bunches of grass up by their roots, "that you and another person were the only two people on a desert island with no help of ever getting rescued."

Calman hated this kind of what-if question. Wasn't he already on his own type of desert island?

"And let's say," she continued, "that one of you is really attractive, gorgeous even, and the other one is butt-ugly. Which one would you want to be?"

"I don't know."

"Pick one. You have to pick one."

"The attractive one, I guess."

"Why?"

Calman thought about the answer he had offered so quickly without thinking. No one had ever called him attractive. Awkward, puny, petite even, which was really insulting for a boy, he thought. At best he was "cute," which was what Cousin Shirley called him at his bar mitzvah after she'd grabbed his neck with both hands, screamed out, *Cahmeer, my little pootch-kee,*" smacked his cheek with two humongous moist lips, and thrust him backward like she was shoving a boat from shore. At worst, he was a pigeon-toed, knock-kneed, thin-limbed, squirrel-faced kid with large pores and stunning Ralph Lauren eyeglasses. "Attractive" was a word for the likes of James Bond. "I don't know," he answered. "Why wouldn't anyone want to be attractive?"

"Me. I'd definitely want to be the ugly one."

"Why?"

"Because A, I don't care what I look like; B, it's definitely easier to be ugly, you don't have to do a damn thing but let your mole hairs grow down to your ankles; C, I'm not looking in any mirror . . . I gotta look at the other person all day long; and D, maybe if I'm ugly the other person would leave me the hell alone and I'd have the whole island to myself."

"Wouldn't you get lonely?"

"No way. I can take care of myself just fine."

Calman didn't get Rizzy. Would she really want to be alone or was she just saying that? She had to be just saying that. She had to, or else she didn't know what it was like to be alone. No one could possibly want to be alone forever, or ugly forever, with long mole hairs, he thought. He and Rizzy should play role-reversal like his therapist tried to get him to do with his parents. The role-reversal game would let her see how lucky she was to have lots of siblings and family around who played with her and kept her mind from wandering into self-harassment.

"Okay," said Calman, "so now imagine it's five years later, and you're still alone. You've been alone all that time, with no one around to talk to or play with. Sal isn't there, or your parents, or anyone, and you know you're going to be alone for your entire life. Close your eyes and tell me how you would feel."

"Close my eyes? Tell you how I would feel? What are you, a psychiatrist? Next you'll be hypnotizing me and making me squawk like a chicken."

"No, I just meant . . ."

"Well, I know how I'd feel. Awesome. No one would be telling me what I could or couldn't do, so I could do anything I wanted. I'd be living the high life."

Calman knew Rizzy must be referring to her mother telling her what to do. He'd witnessed numerous Level Ten arguments between them in the short time he'd been there. Besides being shocked by their frequency and content, Calman was most alarmed and fascinated by their volume, for never before had he heard such screaming. His parents fought, it was true, but their fights built like approaching thunder and broke before voices were inappropriately and unhealthily raised, leaving gray moods in their wake.

Calman had screamed once when he was eight over some TV movie—he couldn't remember which one—that his parents wouldn't let him watch. He had cried with his mouth wide open and had cracked a ceramic bowl on the hardwood floor, splattering raspberry sorbet on the white sheepskin throw rug and the black leather couch, and had been sent to his room. In a groggy state, he had thought he saw his mother standing over his head blowing red-hot fire out her nostrils while she told him he would never do that again. Though he dreamed often of reenacting that same scene with various other stain-making flavors, he obeyed her.

A uniformed man emerged from one of the doors of the prison. He leaned casually against the side of the building and smoked a cigarette. Another car drove by on the road, and all three of them turned to watch it pass. A crow landed on a branch and rustled its leaves in the windless silence. The man threw his cigarette butt to the ground, glanced up toward Rizzy and Calman, then walked back into the building. The glass door closed slowly behind him.

"So how come you didn't ask me why I'm writing smut?" Rizzy flipped over to her back and rested her head on her palms.

"I don't know. Are you writing a book to get published?"

"Not exactly. Can you keep a secret?"

"Yeah."

"Penalty of death if you tell, I swear. Promise?"

"Promise."

Rizzy sat up and moved in closer to Calman, who was leaning against a tree in his yoga position. "I concocted the best practical joke in history on Lily, and she hasn't figured it out yet. It's brilliant."

"What did you do?"

"It's what I'm still doing. Okay, get this. Lily loves romance novels, right? She's probably read every one ever written. She doesn't even go to our local bookstore anymore because she's read everything they have. Plus, she's embarrassed to have anyone see her buy them. She likes to give the impression that she's, you know, above that . . . prim and proper. You saw how she keeps them locked up, as if none of us has ever seen her panting over them in the kitchen corner.

"Anyway, almost a year ago, I got an idea. I went into work one day with Bob and used his computer and color copier to print up a whole package of junk mail marketing mumbo jumbo. I copied stuff from some magazine. It had one of those letters that said something like, 'Dear Fellow Romance Novel Lover . . . Reading behind closed doors? Tired of waiting around for new editions to come out? Well, this offer is for you!' Blah blah blah. Then there was a flyer that said, 'Free 90-day trial. Just mail back the enclosed card and every month you'll receive your prepublished chapter of the hottest new up-coming romance novel, never before seen by anyone else except its author.' And then I put, 'And since it's typewritten on loose pages, your family will think you're reading tax forms or a letter from your best friend. No more hiding those lurid book covers. This is for you!' Is that not brilliant?"

"But where would she send the card back to?"

"That didn't matter. I made up some address in New York."

"I don't get it."

"Just listen, butt-head. I put everything in a big envelope and mailed it to her with some made-up return address label. 'Romance Novel Distribution' is the name I used, which was another stroke of genius, but I'll explain that in a minute. You should have seen me, I was all sun and roses. 'Oh, Lily,' I said, 'looks like you got some mail.' Then I watched her open it. I pretended to be doing something else, but I watched her. She read it, devoured it, I'd say, and immediately marked the card

'Yes' and put it near the front door with the pile of mail to be sent. So I didn't need the card. See? I knew it was a go. I knew she'd fall for it hook, line, and sinker."

"So how do you know what to write?"

"Easy. Like I told you, I've read all her books. The plot, the language . . . all formula. I just use the same words. Sometimes I even steal whole paragraphs; she doesn't notice. Woman with big breasts meets handsome stud with big biceps. Only the setting and circumstances change. Beach, ski lodge, whatever. As long as the stud is, as they say, 'well endowed,' and the chick wins him in the end, Lily's on cloud nine."

Well endowed. Calman didn't exactly know what that meant, but he'd heard it before. His father had used that term once when they were in a department store dressing room trying on underpants. Because he had refused to go into the women's dressing rooms with his mother since his age had reached double digits, he accompanied his father into the men's area and promised to try the new underpants on over the ones he was already wearing, even though he wasn't supposed to. This made him look bulbous around those parts and his father had commented with a wink, "Well, well. For a little guy, you're pretty well endowed. You must take after me." When he got home he looked up "well endowed" in the dictionary. It wasn't there, so he looked up "endow." It said: "to provide with a source of income." Given where his father was looking when he made that comment, Calman had thought maybe his penis would make him rich one day, though he hadn't felt imaginative enough to figure out how.

"Anyway," continued Rizzy, "she still doesn't know it's me."

"Doesn't she hear you typing all the time?"

"That's the beauty of it. She thinks I'm writing to you. That's why I got a pen pal. Having a pen pal was the perfect alibi."

That stung. So all this time she didn't really want to be pen pals, she was just using him. Their friendship was a sham. Lies, all lies. He didn't want to hear about her mother anymore, he wanted to go home, home to Boston. Suddenly, all of this felt like too much information to process.

"Of course," said Rizzy, "I don't know what she thinks I'm typing now that you're here, but who cares. Princess-Not-So-Bright hasn't figured it out yet and she won't. Man, you should see the way she grabs for it when it comes in the mail. 'What's that?' I always ask innocently. 'Oh, nothing, dear,' she says, and hides it behind her back.

"Oh, and I didn't tell you the best part. She paid me to do it! After ninety days, you know, when the free offer was up, I sent her a bill for a year's subscription at ninety-six dollars, that's just eight dollars a month, I said. Just eight dollars a month! And here's the best part—I had her write out a check to 'RND,' which obviously stood for Romance Novel Distribution, but what she didn't realize was that it also stands for Rosalita Nell Dickson. So I grabbed the check and filled in my name after the initials. It was a tight fit, and maybe a little suspect, but I knew I wouldn't have a problem cashing it. One of the bank tellers is a friend of Grandpa's, so I let him in on the joke. He loved it, of course, and helped me cash the check. The hardest part was grabbing the cashed check when it came back. I didn't even know checks came back until I saw it on the kitchen table. She doesn't balance her checkbook, so she didn't even notice it was missing."

Calman didn't say anything. He wanted to yell out that he didn't care. He didn't want to know any more about anything if that was how she felt about being pen pals.

"Hello? You want to know what I'm going to do with it?"

"No."

Rizzy tightened her eyebrows and leaned into Calman's face. "What's wrong with you?"

"Nothing."

"Nothing what? What'd I say?"

"Nothing." Calman looked the other way. He threw a rock at a flower bed, but it fell far short of its target and disappeared into the grass. "Just for the record," he said quietly, "I didn't want a pen pal either."

"Oh, I get it." Rizzy threw a rock in the same direction. It hit the building. "Listen, don't be stupid. I could have pretended to have a pen pal, right? I still wrote to you, right?"

Calman shrugged his shoulders. She had a point. "So you didn't just write to me because you had to?"

"At first I did, but I don't know. You amused me."

Rizzy sidled up next to him. Now they both leaned against the tree, side by side, her bent knee gently bumping his every now and again in an uncharacteristically gentle manner. "I invited you here, didn't I, dumb-ass?" She bumped her shoulder up against his shoulder, let the tip of her sneaker touch his sneaker. "Are you sorry you came?"

"No."

"Well, then."

In a moment like this, he felt bold. "Rizzy," he said softly, "why do you fight so much with your mother?"

Rizzy looked away before she answered. "She's not my mother."

"You mean you're adopted?"

"Yeah, I'm adopted. My mother was a beautiful Navajo Indian and my father was a chief, but I haven't seen them since the white man stole me away and sold me to some missionaries, who sold me again at a church auction. Lily was the highest bidder. She thought she was buying a doll, something she could dress up and parade around town. Needless to say, she was in for a rude awakening."

What's the difference, thought Calman, between truth and fiction if you don't actually know which is which? How would you know a lie was a lie if the person telling you the lie said it was the truth? People more often told you that what they were saying was the truth, for no one really said something outright and then said, "I'm lying." So truth was the trickier one. Lies were lies, but truths could be truths or lies. And if you didn't really know whether the truth was the real truth or whether it was a lie, then maybe you would have to rely on other clues.

Calman thought about the other clues. First, he had caught Rizzy in several lies, so he could assume that she lied a lot. Second, if Lily popped out babies like a leaky faucet, why would she have to buy a baby? She had to have made it up. *Why? Why did she make that up? What is she hiding?* said his therapist in his head. *There are truths in lies.* He never really understood when his therapist said that. Once, he had complained that when his parents went out at night, they always said they'd be home soon or they wouldn't be late, but they never came home soon and they were always too late to tuck him in and say good night. In other words, they lied. *Perhaps the truth was that they didn't want to worry you, to add to your anxiety.* To Calman, that meant that because of who he was, he had caused his parents to lie. Maybe, he pondered, he had that effect on others. Maybe he caused Rizzy to lie, too.

"Why are you so quiet? You don't believe me?"

"Well, I guess," he said. "It's just . . . I was thinking. You owe me a truth, from the game, remember? I was just wondering if you would still give the same answer if it was a truth question in the game."

It looked like she was going to say something, but she didn't. She looked at him and then she looked in every direction but at him.

Calman felt sorry for her. "Never mind," he said. "It's okay."

She stood up. "C'mon," she said. "I want to show you some-thing."

They rode for a time on the open road, parting the vast sun-beaten air with 300, going on 301, 302, 303 rotations of their pedals. Calman tried to keep up with Rizzy, counting to him-self so he wouldn't give up, and wouldn't obsess about getting farther and farther away from where they would have to even-tually get back to before it got dark. They turned off the main road and finally the houses and trees they passed were close enough together that they blocked the sun. Calman welcomed the shade, as it signaled the comforting palpability of civiliza-tion. There were parked cars, sidewalks, even a few people.

Rizzy led him into the thick of the neighborhood, until Calman could no longer tell from which direction they had come. He pedaled hard to avoid losing sight of her while he thought of ways he could mark their trail. Not popcorn—Cal-man had always thought that was stupid—but rocks or sticks or something inconspicuous. There was a time when he used to carry around chalk for writing on trees in case he was kid-napped.

Rizzy stopped and stood, straddling her bike. Calman glided close to where she stood and did the same. He bent his head down over his handlebars and caught his breath. When he looked up, he noticed she was staring at the house in front of them.

"Whose house is this?" asked Calman.

"This is where I used to live."

The small house was cramped between two other houses. It was covered with chipped blue paint and bird droppings, and stood to the right of a rusted carport. There were faded shades drawn over the windows and weeds in the flowerpots on the porch. In front of the house was an old tricycle and a mailbox painted to look like a cow. A neglected garden in front sprouted crumpled beer cans and dog droppings.

"How long ago was that?"

"About six years ago," said Rizzy.

Calman tried to imagine what it would have been like to live here, in a house, instead of in a city apartment. He tried to picture Rizzy at eight years old, playing catch with Larry, running in and out of the front door with Sal. He remembered what Sal had said about how Rizzy used to be happy here. "Does anyone live here now?" he asked.

"Who knows? Who cares?" Rizzy got back on her bike and pedaled slowly toward a large brick building on the corner of the street.

"Riz!" yelled Calman, hurrying to catch up.

The building looked to be at least four or five stories high and wide enough for a large circular driveway. Stone steps led up to the main entrance, above which a sign read VISITORS ENTER HERE. PATIENTS USE SIDE DOOR. The grass around the building looked inviting, but was enclosed and protected by a cold metal gate.

Calman dropped his bike and stood next to Rizzy. Though he didn't notice anything special about the place, he did notice a sudden change in Rizzy's manner. She was staring with frightening intensity at the building's entrance.

"What is this place?"

"This gate wasn't here before," said Rizzy. Her muscles were taut, her knuckles in tight fists around the gate's bars were nearly white.

Rizzy turned and looked at him, but she didn't see him. She was far away. She spoke quickly. "Did you know Lily's a murderer? She killed someone right there, right in front of where we're standing. It was a little girl in a wheelchair. Lily walked up, stuck a knife right in her heart, let her bleed to death, and walked away." Rizzy suddenly shook the gate wildly until the whole length of it vibrated in a resounding cacophony of clanking metal. *"Just . . . walked . . . a . . . way,"* she yelled over the clanging. And then she stopped. A few faces appeared in the windows of some of the building's upper floors, and then receded.

Calman felt a pang of pity for Rizzy. This was a lie with truths, Calman knew. She was feeling real anger—Level Ten anger for sure—and though he didn't know what had really happened here or what she was angry about, he felt the part of him without words understood the part of her without words, and it had to do with mothers who make their sons and daughters inhale when all they want to do is exhale.

"My mother killed someone, too," he lied. "He was my

babysitter. He misbehaved, and to teach him a lesson she locked him in a box. The box had air holes on the top, but she forgot he was in there and she sat on the box for a long time and he suffocated to death."

Rizzy let go of the gate and faced him. The edges of her lips rose into a devilish grin. "You suck as a liar, you know that, don't you?"

Calman smiled. He leaned against the gate and concentrated on the sun. Despite the well-known warnings, he looked directly at the sun and then closed his eyes, enjoying the white blindness that blanketed the rest of the visible world. He felt the sun's warmth on his legs and his arms and his face, and the hard ground underneath him and the flimsy gate behind him, and in that cocoonlike moment he suddenly felt something else, something moist and mushy on his lips. He popped open his eyes and saw Rizzy's eyes, watching his eyes, but she was so close that he was cross-eyed, and couldn't see anything that wasn't blurry, and he could feel a little puff of air from her nostrils and could taste her tongue when it rolled around his tongue and could smell orange ChapStick on her lips because they were pressed against his lips and when it dawned on him that she was kissing him—that this was a kiss!—that this was a real mouth-to-mouth kiss—his first kiss!—he gasped into her mouth so that she jumped back and coughed.

"What are you doing, giving me mouth-to-mouth resuscitation?"

"What did you do that for?" That was the only thing Calman could think of saying at the moment. Apparently, it didn't go over very well with Rizzy, for she backed up immediately and picked up her bike.

"Do what?" she said.

"That."

"That what?"

"You kissed me." He was defensive by accident and now she was defensive and that was not what was supposed to be happening.

"Did not. You're dreaming."

"I felt it. I saw you." What he meant to say was, Wow. What he meant to say was, Thank You and Wow and Was it okay? Did I do it right? Did you like it? Did you feel something? Is this your first kiss, too? Do you think I'm attractive? Can I tell the world? Can I tell my therapist? Can we keep it a secret between you and me? Will you do it again? Are you my girlfriend now? Will I remember this when I'm old?

"I wouldn't kiss you if you were the last man on earth," said Rizzy. "Besides," she added as she began to pedal away, "you kiss like a girl."

And Bingo Was His Name-O

Tuesday and much of Wednesday passed quickly. Rizzy and Calman spent time downtown reading in the corners of bookstores, listening to street music, drinking smoothies, seeing a mildly funny computer-animated movie. Rizzy never mentioned the kiss, so neither did Calman, though he thought a lot about it and wondered if he'd be able to kiss Rizzy again before he left. Rizzy still played the occasional prank and tried to spook him every now and again, but mostly she was easier to be with, and for the first time since he left home, Calman felt he was glad he came.

On Wednesday evening, Simon said Calman was in for a treat. He was going to take him, along with Rizzy and Sal, to play bingo. He played every Wednesday, Rizzy said, and now that school was over, he'd been taking her and Sal along with him. The drive was an easy five minutes from the house.

"Have you ever played before?" Sal asked as they walked to the door of the American Legion. He had a bounce to his step and kept jumping up and shooting imaginary basketballs.

Calman tried to keep stride with him. "No. I mean, I know what it is, but I never really played. Will you tell me what to do?"

"Yeah, sure. It's not hard."

"Wait till you see what these people bring with them," said Rizzy. "They're the weirdest bunch of—"

"Now, now," said Simon. "We all got our quirks." He held the front door open for them. "Why, look at me, look at the weird things I'm bringing in, I got 'em *all* beat," he joked, smacking Rizzy on the behind.

The game hall was a large, wood-paneled room with three long tables. Several people waved to Simon before he went into a side room to buy bingo cards. Calman, Rizzy, and Sal surveyed the scene. A game was already in progress. There were about fifty people: some families, but mostly older players. Calman thought he recognized one or two of them from the Saturday morning diner crowd.

"That's called a blower," said Sal, pointing at the forced-air device mixing the bingo balls at the front. "And he's the caller." The man who pulled a ball from the blower wore a black suit too small for his paunch. His visor sported several colorful pins, and half his fingers were adorned with large gold rings. There was a constant low murmuring of voices until his bellowing cry boomed through the room.

"N forty-four. Droopy drawers. Open doors. What a bore. N forty-four."

There was sudden movement among the players and eruptions of glee or disappointment. Hands with what looked like big ink daubers got busy stamping. Most players had several cards going at once, which made the whole game seem too fast and difficult to follow.

"Check this out," said Rizzy, pointing to the table. "Look at what these freaks call good luck charms."

Calman thought of his grandmother and the way her lips looked when she said the word *chotchkis*. That's what she would call what he saw lined up in each player's space: little trolls with wild hair, photos of grandchildren, ceramic figurines. "Do they work?" he asked. He wasn't one to knock good luck charms. He had several himself.

"Well, they obviously don't work for everyone if everyone has them, right?" said Rizzy.

"O seventy-one!" cried the caller. "O seventy-one. Bang on the drum. Bum ditty bum. Number seventy-one."

"Bingo!" a woman up front screamed. "I got Bingo!"

There were oohs and ahs and other vowel sounds from the room until a man verified her card, and then the players clapped.

Simon returned and the four of them took seats in the corner.

"Hey, that's my seat. Don't you sit there," said a small man with a long pointy nose and big ears. He looked like a rodent.

"Sorry," said Calman, standing and sliding the chair back. The seat looked unoccupied to him. "I didn't know this was your seat."

"Well, it is," said the odd man.

"Here, son," said Simon, making room for him by moving down one seat and having Rizzy and Sal do the same.

"That guy's a mental case," whispered Rizzy as they sat. "God forbid anyone should take his *lucky* seat."

Calman, now seated between Rizzy and the rodent, draped his sweatshirt over his chair. Rizzy had made fun of him for bringing it, but he didn't care. He had been freezing in the movie theater the day before and didn't want to chance it again, but thankfully it was comfortably warm in the game hall. He took his cards and ink dauber from Simon and got ready to play. Simon, Sal, and Rizzy were all playing several cards, but Calman wanted just one for now.

"Eyes down," said the caller, "all eyes down."

"Here we go," said Rizzy.

The caller pulled a ball from the blower. "Lucky seven. God's in heaven. Snow White's brethren. B seven."

Calman didn't have a seven. In fact, he didn't have the next several numbers called, and eventually he lost the game. So did

Rizzy, Sal, and Simon. It was a man at another table who called Bingo.

"Was that Bud?" said Simon. He turned around and said more loudly, "Bud, was that you?"

"Sure was!" Bud yelled back.

"Well, all right," said Simon, putting away his cards and getting new ones out.

"You still going to play one card?" Rizzy asked Calman.

"For now," said Calman. Because he was playing on only one card he had time to look around and lament the fact that he wasn't part of a community like this. He wasn't thinking of these people in particular, or even people like them—the rodent kept scowling at him every time he coughed—but a community of regulars who came every week and knew your name and waved hello when you walked in or patted you on the back when you won and asked what you're going to buy for your wife, whose name they also knew. Mrs. Blenke had her Mah-Jongg group, and even Sal was out bowling with his buddies the night before, as he did every week. Calman didn't have a community of people like that. He didn't think his parents did either. The best they had was dinner guests.

"Eyes down," said the caller, "eyes down."

The evening passed quickly, and before long Simon was telling them this would be their last game. Calman gave it a shot with two boards. Rizzy and Sal were playing on four. They listened to the caller.

"I thirty. Dirty Gertie. Flirty thirty. Ain't you perty little thirty."

Calman said *yes* under his breath in triumph and blotted the number thirty on both of his boards.

"You suck," said Rizzy.

The caller cried out again, and now both Rizzy and the rodent were grumbling. The rodent had five ink daubers standing up in a row to his right and, to his left, three bobbing heads of past presidents. "C'mon, fifty-six," he said with desperation, "Fifty-six, fifty-six, fifty-six!" He patted the head of President Nixon.

"I twenty-two. Dinky doo. Desmond Tutu. I twenty-two."

"Ach," said the rodent, and laid President Nixon facedown on the table in disgust.

"It's about time," said Rizzy.

With the next several numbers Rizzy got lucky, until it looked like she was really close to winning.

"O seventy-five. Top of the house. As far as we go. End of the line. O seventy-five."

"Bingo!" yelled Rizzy. She yelled so loudly that Calman jumped and sent his ink dauber flying onto the next table. *Was it true? She really won?*

A man came over and held up her board. "Yup," he said. "We have a winner."

Everyone clapped. Calman was proud to be sitting next to her. Rizzy stood up, and because Calman was right next to her, his face now close to her tan shorts when she turned and took a bow, he saw something he wished he hadn't seen. He knew what it was, too. He stopped clapping.

155

"Riz," he said. She sat back down.

"Way to go, Riz," said Sal. "You probably got fifty bucks. You should treat us all to ice cream." He collected his used cards and said he'd meet them outside.

Simon congratulated Rizzy and then started talking to the people behind him. Calman had to try harder to get her attention.

"Rizzy!" he said, more loudly.

"What?"

He hesitated. "Don't you have to go to the bathroom?" He sounded like his mother.

"No," she said, looking at him strangely.

He glanced down at her shorts and then back at her eyes. He couldn't see the bloodstain now that she was sitting down and facing him, but he knew others would see it the minute she got up, if they hadn't already. "I think you should go to the bathroom." He spoke more slowly this time, hoping his hints would get through.

Rizzy searched his face until she understood, and with a swift, loud push of her chair she ran to the bathroom.

When she didn't come back after a while, Simon asked Calman where she went. "To the bathroom," he said. "But she probably went outside. I'll go find her."

"Fine, fine. I'll take her board and pick up her winnings."

Calman found her in the hallway where they came in. She had her back to the wall. He was expecting her to be seething mad, to lash out at him for one reason or another, to do something crazy, but when he approached her, all she did was look away. He could see she was breathing heavy. *Had she been crying?* Her cheeks looked a little flushed. It was a side of her he hadn't seen before, and it was both uncomfortable and wonderful.

"There you are," said Simon, coming back in from outside. "Sal and I were looking for you two. Rizzy, you got sixty bucks, kid! Sal insists you treat us to ice cream."

"I just want to go home," she said softly.

"What's the matter, darlin'?" He leaned in to her.

"Nothing."

"Well, then, let's go celebrate. C'mon, now." Simon patted her on the shoulder and then headed outside.

When it became clear to Calman that she didn't want to move away from the wall, he got an idea.

"Here," he said, holding out his sweatshirt. "Take it."

She looked at it, and then at him.

"Really," he said. "Just take it."

She reached out to accept his gift and wrapped it around her waist. "Thanks," she said warmly, and they walked out together.

1 Lost My Poor Meatball

Calman—along with Rizzy, Lily, and Simon—spotted Tank's exposed butt crack near the bottom shelf of the pet-food aisle at the local grocery store. Tank had been on all fours, unsticking and resticking the products' tiny white price tags to his advantage, when he noticed he was being watched. He stood with great effort and shook hands with Simon. A strip of hazy sunshine sliced his torso and illuminated the stains on his white cotton undershirt.

"Well, now, roll-it-up-a-notch, tonight is 'Cops' night," he replied to Simon's dinner invitation. "If I'm going to miss quality TV, it'd better roll-it-up-a-notch be good." Piped in over the ringing cash registers and clanking carts was a DJ from the local oldies station promising a commercial-free hour of music.

"It's up to you," said Simon. "We're having meatballs and some fine feminine company, if you get my meaning."

Something about Tank's demeanor and general disregard for proper hygiene reminded Calman of the heavyset man he'd seen on the plane who took enormously deep breaths and walked sideways down the aisle. They both had the same repulsive habit of blowing their noses and then examining the very spots on their handkerchiefs at which they had aimed.

"A lady? Why roll-it-up-a-notch didn't you say so? Course I'll roll-it-up-a-notch be there." Tank picked out a rag from his cart and used it to wipe the sweat from his brow. His rounded belly became visible as he hitched up the back end of his pants. "Much obliged," he said, and smiled at Lily, who managed a polite nod.

"He's gross," said Rizzy after Tank had said goodbye and waddled toward the freezer section. "He might as well just make a mustache out of those big ol' nose hairs."

Calman laughed quietly. Rizzy was back to her old self.

"For heaven's sake, Daddy. Did you have to do that?" added Lily as the four of them walked through the fruit and vegetable section.

"I'm just being neighborly is all." Simon was scratching his beard and picking at the grapes Lily had taken five minutes to select.

"What could you have been thinking of? Such a long time it's been since we've entertained any guests and you have to go and ruin everything," Lily said, lowering her voice.

"Lily, your dinner party'd go just fine if you'd just relax. Ain't nobody going to misbehave . . . though a little misbe-havin' would be okay with me. Hoo-wee. That Eleanor—"

"That's enough," said Lily, a little too loudly. A woman with two onions in her hand eyed her suspiciously over her bifocals. "There are children present."

"Where?" asked Rizzy, who had been nonchalantly placing random items into Lily's cart, like ointment for hemorrhoids. "Prevents flare-ups," she whispered to Calman as she hid it under the laundry detergent.

Simon chuckled at Lily's knack for melodrama and tipped his hat at the onion lady. Then he winked at Calman with one of his hazel eyes. Calman loved it when he did that. He loved that Simon connected with him with such a seemingly innocuous, though powerfully intimate, gesture. Calman at times found himself studying Simon with surreptitious glances—the way his beard appeared dense and pepper-colored in places, and how he puckered his lips when he was pensive or sly. He wondered if his own grandfather had been a winker, before he died of pneumonia when Calman was just two. Calman remembered looking in a dusty photo album at a frayed picture of himself on his grandfather's lap, above which someone had written "the terrible twos." Based on his mother's explanation that he'd been "a little horror" during that dark period of his life, he had always assumed that his unfortunate phase of development had somehow contributed to his grandfather's demise.

"Cal," said the supermarket cashier. Calman returned his attention to his surroundings now that they were checking out and stared at the boy who'd called his name. "Your sister's been calling to you . . . by the door." He pointed at Rizzy, who had slipped outside and was motioning for Calman to follow.

"She's not my sister," said Calman, but the cashier didn't hear him. The register had flung open its bottom lip and he was busy counting change. Calman was disturbed that the cashier assumed he and Rizzy had a familial relationship. Why couldn't he be her boyfriend? What does a boyfriend look like? "I'm her boyfriend," he said, trying out the words.

"Yeah, right. You wish," the cashier said with a snicker.

"Daddy, please don't," said Lily, for Simon had finished bagging the groceries and had begun juggling two apples.

Simon stopped juggling and, with a devilish grin, offered her one of the apples.

"Would Eve like a little bite?" he asked, hissing through his middle teeth.

"Give me that," snapped Lily as she nudged Calman toward the door. "God help us," she mumbled. Calman hung his head and followed her outside.

By seven o'clock, one half hour before the dinner guests were scheduled to arrive, the air in the Dicksons' kitchen smelled like a slightly rancid blend of food, heat, and perspiration. Every light in the house was on, and every vase, picture, couch, and corner had been dusted more than once. Without toys and clothing strewn about the hallways, the younger children had found space for cartwheels and somersaults; they were particularly excited and therefore hyperactive over the thought of having company for dinner.

"Francesca, stop that. Did you put your things away in your room? Go do that right now. My Lord, why I ever thought I could do this." Lily shuffled her children up the stairs, wiped her brow, and took a deep breath as she surveyed the living room. She moved about like a pinball, straightening, fixing, and backing up to see what her guests would see as they came through the door.

"Robert, you scared me," said Lily as she swirled around suddenly to see her husband standing in the doorway. He had a T-shirt on with sweat stains under the armpits. "Where have you been? Why haven't you changed? Is the doorbell fixed? *Well, is it?*"

The red blotches on Lily's cheeks and neck were now prominent eyesores. Bob stared at her and offered a comforting smile, as if he had successfully built up an immunity to Lily's neuroses over the years.

"Doorbell's fixed, kids are getting ready, and I'm headed upstairs to put on that nice blue shirt you picked out for me for my birthday. All right on schedule," he said as he walked over to Lily and gave her a kiss on her pink forehead. "It's going to be just fine," he whispered.

"I'll tell you, Robert, I just wish . . ." she began when the doorbell rang.

"I'll get it," yelled Rizzy, who came barreling down the

stairs with bare feet. Calman watched from an opening in the dining room.

"Oh, my Lord, Robert, they're early. Robert!" Lily scooted around Bob and checked herself in the tiny mirror by the front door. She patted her hair, untied her apron, and took one last look around the house. Rizzy and Lily peeked around the door as they opened it slowly and deliberately.

"Evenin'," said Tank, leaning into the screen. Rizzy and Lily examined his appearance. He wore a light green sports coat and had slicked back his dark hair so that it shone brightly in the reflected light. In one hand he held a box of Santa Claus–shaped chocolates, and in the other a bottle of whiskey.

"Oh, it's you," said Rizzy and Lily together, surprising each other.

"You're early, Tank," said Lily politely. "Come in." Tank stepped into the hallway and handed her the whiskey.

"Meatballs and whiskey," he said. "Goes together roll-it-up-a-notch like pork and beans." Lily masked her disgust with urbane appreciation and stared down at the box of chocolates under his dirty fingernails.

"Yes, well, and look at ol' Saint Nick," said Lily, pointing to the chocolates. "Never too early for Christmas, I always say," she said somewhat cheerfully.

"She always says that," said Rizzy sarcastically. She was swinging from the doorknob with her feet planted wide apart on either side of the door.

"Rosalita, let go of that. Your father just fixed that door.

Now, go see what your brothers are doing." Lily placed the chocolates and whiskey on a shelf under the mirror by the front door to free her hands. She put her apron back on and buttoned the top few buttons of her peach-colored dress. "Daddy!" she yelled with some urgency in no particular direction. "Where is he? Daddy! Company's here! Tank, why don't you have a seat." She pointed to the living room and eyed him nervously. Tank bowed slightly, clapped his fleshy hands together, and walked over to the fireplace.

In contrast to the yelps and thumps and general activity upstairs, the downstairs area had suddenly filled with the uncomfortable silence of two people who have nothing to say to each other. Tank smiled at Lily. Lily smiled at Tank. They both fidgeted with their fingers and breathed heavily.

"Daddy!" she yelled again.

Tank looked past Lily to see if Simon was anywhere near, and happened to notice Calman in the doorway between the kitchen and living room. Calman had been observing Tank from afar since his arrival. Now he flushed under Tank's gaze.

"Hello there, roll-it-up-a-notch," said Tank, stretching forward over his feet to see him. Calman kept his distance and raised his palm in a half wave.

"Well, you'll excuse me," said Lily. "I should go check on dinner. Calman, why don't you keep our guest company. Tank, make yourself comfortable."

The trim of Lily's dress brushed Calman's knees as she hurried to the kitchen. Calman watched the movement of her hands as she went, how they tucked and pulled and smoothed to try and hide her plump figure. She reached the stove and stood with her back to Calman. Her breathing showed in the quickened rise and fall of her shoulders, as if each intake of air were an arduous attempt to defy gravity. Her hands were still moving, now grabbing at objects: a spoon, a pot, a bottle of pills. Calman watched as her head popped back in a sudden jerk and her free hand reached for a glass of water. Perhaps, he thought, he should be polite and ask her if she needed any help.

"Where you going?" Tank blurted out. Calman stopped abruptly and turned to him. "You're that roll-it-up-a-notch Boston boy, ain't ya?"

With all of Tank's weight on one side of the couch, the opposite end of the long cushion underneath him rose in the air like a seesaw. It seemed implausible that Tank could get up from his seat quickly, which prompted Calman to entertain the idea of making a run for it.

"Come on in here for a minute roll-it-up-a-notch. I ain't gonna bite."

Calman did as he was told and walked slowly into the living room. He stood across from Tank and leaned against the wall, still close to the hallway.

"How old are you, son?"

"Thirteen," said Calman in a barely audible mumble. Lily dropped something metal on a hard surface and they both turned toward the kitchen.

"Fifteen?"

"No, thirteen," Calman repeated with more confidence.

"Oh, thirteen roll-it-up-a-notch." Tank shook his head. "Just a bitty teenager. Can't even remember when I roll-it-up-a-notch was thirteen. Long time ago. I was somewhere here 'n eastern Washington, I know that roll-it-up-a-notch, but hell if I know exactly where. I was always roll-it-up-a-notch moving around some as a child. No house ever good enough for my old man. Well, that's what he used to say anyhow. Prob'ly never paid the rent roll-it-up-a-notch is more likely, may he rest in peace. Say, how much do you weigh?"

Calman had trouble focusing on anything but *roll-it-up-a-notch*. How did a person get stuck with a hiccup like that? What did it mean? Had it once been a full sentence that got squeezed into a tight space? Calman wondered why no one ever said anything to Tank.

"I say, how much roll-it-up-a-notch do you weigh?"

"Oh, I don't know."

"You're a skinny little fellow roll-it-up-a-notch for a teenager. I must've weighed two, three times what you do when I was your age. Had the football physique roll-it-up-a-notch from the get-go. Wasn't nobody in the school roll-it-up-a-notch that could knock me down, though they all tried, of course. I always told them roll-it-up-a-notch they ought to pick on someone their own size, that is, if they wanted to live." Tank's laugh set his whole football physique in motion and made him sweat.

Calman stared at Tank's cheeks, which had a glossy shine to them as if they were covered in Saran wrap. He knew exactly what Tank had been like at his age. There were always Tanks in Calman's school, in every grade, in every class. They filled their seats and half of yours at assemblies, and pushed open your bathroom stall door with little effort. Unlike true bullies, though, Calman had found that the Tanks of the world could usually be won over with a few chocolate bars.

"Say, you're not superstitious, are you?"

"I don't think so," said Calman.

"Good, 'cause there are some that'd say roll–it–up–a–notch that thirteen is an unlucky number. Take my ex-wife. She wouldn't even say the number out loud. Eleven, twelve, a baker's dozen, she'd say. Ten and three. Never a mention until her dying day when I swear to you it was on the thirteenth can of beer roll–it–up–a–notch that she keeled over, and if that isn't already stranger than fiction roll–it–up–a–notch she died on the thirteenth of April. I always thought that her tombstone should read 'See, I told you so,' roll–it–up–a–notch, but a friend of mine pointed out that that was thirteen letters roll–it–up–a–notch and I'd better not push it if I wanted to see her in heaven. We had a good laugh over that one."

This thirteen business explained a lot to Calman, who suddenly felt weak in the knees.

"You a gambler?"

"No." Calman had had enough of this small talk. He felt tired and slightly ill, and something about Tank's voice was beginning to sound more and more like the voice of his therapist. His bad luck was becoming excruciatingly apparent.

"Yeah, horses are my weakness," continued Tank. "Got a tip on Hell's Fire in the fifth this evening roll-it-up-a-notch. We'll see how the night goes, eh?"

A square Formica table had been unfolded and placed symmetrically in the center of the kitchen. While the evening's guests congregated in the living room for hors d'oeuvres, the younger Dickson children sat noisily in the kitchen and spotted the table with the red smears of an early spaghetti dinner. By circumventing Lily and asking Bob and Simon first, Rizzy and Calman won the right to stay up later than the other children and join in the dinner party. After all, it was Calman's last night. He was disappointed that Sal was sleeping at a friend's house for the night, even though Sal said he'd be back to say goodbye. Calman felt somewhat ready to go, but he didn't want to say goodbye to Sal. He daydreamed about taking Sal home with him to be *his* brother.

Lily said she wanted her children up to bed and out of the way before the adults sat down to what she hoped would be an "epicurean delight to the senses." She even proposed to dress Francesca in an adorable little French maid's outfit and supply her with a bell to encourage people into the dining room and tell them, after a clearing of the throat to get their attention, "Dinner is served." But Bob nixed the idea before Lily's machinations formed into complete sentences.

"Why don't *you* wear the little maid's outfit," said Rizzy between the pink explosions of her bubble-gum bubbles. "You know you want to."

"No one asked for your opinion, young lady." Lily relaxed her scowl after a quick glance at Calman and then dismissed the situation with a sigh. "Oh, Robert. You're such a fuddy-duddy."

"You tell him," said Rizzy.

Calman was excited to see Mrs. Blenke, if one could ever label any feeling he had as "excitement." The time before her arrival seemed to last forever, then she actually walked through the door, and he suddenly wished he had had more time to prepare. She wore a bright red dress, black pumps, sheer stockings, and a black cowboy hat. On the plane she had looked, even smelled, to Calman like a grandmother. He had thought of her as old and weary, and thus comforting and sexless. But in church, and now tonight, she looked like a different woman. He hadn't noticed before her delicate figure, her defined shoulders, and the shine in her silver hair. The days since their arrival seemed to have removed years from her appearance and given her a certain charm, which Calman found somewhat disquieting.

Still, though he had known her for only a short time, he had missed her, more than his own mother, strangely enough. He had missed the smell of her rose-scented hand cream and her neighborhood gossip about people both foreign to him and yet strangely familiar. Her voice had stayed with him, in his head, and often lulled him to sleep like a glass of warm milk.

But he knew it wouldn't be like that tonight. He wouldn't have her to himself. He had to share her with Tank's dirty jokes and Lily's high-pitched small talk and Simon's flirtatious advances and with everyone else who couldn't understand what she really was: a woman who would never send a young boy away on his own while she flew off to Florida.

"Alvin, I dare say you look like you got some color in those cheeks of yours." Mrs. Blenke cradled Calman's chin in her palm and smiled. He was sitting below her on the floor, close to the doorway and at the opposite end of the couch from Tank. Tank was busy trying to entertain Rizzy with a deck of cards he had pulled from his inside pocket.

Mrs. Blenke cleared her throat. "So did you have a good time in Walla Walla?" she asked Calman politely. "That is," she said softly, leaning toward him as if to share a secret, "did you have an adventure?"

"Oh, Calman has been having a wonderful time, haven't you, dear?" Lily interjected before Calman had a chance to fully ponder the question. Lily had unfolded an extra chair and positioned it in the middle of the living room across from Mrs. Blenke. She sat with her hands placed neatly in the folds of her thighs.

"He and the children have been so active. So much to do on a vacation away from home, when everything is new and different, isn't that right, Calman? Of course, he never quite got used to the dry heat out here, but then again, I don't think any of us has ever gotten used to the heat. The sun can be so strong. Pâté, Eleanor?" Lily paused long enough to stand and offer the hors d'oeuvres tray to Mrs. Blenke. There was a choice of yellow butter balls, orange cheese chunks, or brown liver pâté spread on melba toast. Calman studied the tray with his hand over his mouth and nose as if a foul odor had entered the room. "Speaking of vacations," continued Lily as she sat down again, "how often do you get to visit Walla Walla, Eleanor?" Lily raised her hand and patted her hair, rubbed her neck, ran her finger across her lips. Calman felt like telling her to sit still. She was making him nervous. *You're fidgeting, Calman. Is something on your mind?* It seemed like every therapy session he'd been to began with that question.

"A few times a year," answered Mrs. Blenke. "Oscar comes to Seattle every now and again, too. Where is he anyway?"

"Bob's showing him around the house," answered Rizzy, now widening the conversation to include the magician and his frustrated audience. Calman had been watching Rizzy grow more annoyed with each new trick Tank insisted on demonstrating.

"Well roll-it-up-a-notch, I'll take one of those cheese thingamabobs," said Tank. He leaned over Mrs. Blenke's knee and shoveled a few cheese cubes into his palm.

Rizzy crawled away from Tank and wobbled into a headstand. "Tank, show Lily that card trick you just did." Rizzy used her left foot to point at the cards in his hands.

"Oh, you're going to like this one roll-it-up-a-notch. It's my favorite," said Tank with a full mouth. "Here, pick a card." He took his deck and fanned the cards out across the table in front of Lily.

"Oh, my Lord," gasped Lily. She stood up and turned her back to her guests. Calman peered over at the table. Each card he saw had a photograph of a naked woman sprawled in some way or another across silk sheets.

"I . . . I think I better go look for Robert. Dinner is almost ready." Lily pointed to the hallway and quickly backed out of the room.

Tank apologized to Mrs. Blenke, who said she'd seen too much of the world to be offended by a deck of playing cards. Rizzy was not so forgiving.

"You should be ashamed of yourself. In front of the children!" she exclaimed, rolling out of her headstand. Her cheeks were a soft pink. "I . . . I think I better go check on dinner," she said mockingly as she patted her hair and exited the room with Lily's familiar gait. "C'mon, Cal," she yelled from the kitchen.

Calman rose and left Mrs. Blenke and Tank in the living room just as Simon came in the front door carrying his banjo.

"Lily would give her right arm to be nude on a deck of cards. She'll be dreaming about it tonight, believe me," Rizzy was saying to Calman as he positioned himself by the kitchen door. Rizzy was by the stove, stirring a big pot with a long spoon. "Cal, open that cabinet over there and take out the hot sauce on the second shelf."

Calman looked at her, then toward the cabinet behind the table where Rizzy's siblings sat. "There?" he asked. Rizzy nodded. He opened the correct door, moved aside a box of cornflakes, and searched among the various bottles.

"Hurry. Lily will be back any minute."

"This one?" He raised a bottle in the air.

"Yeah, yeah. Bring it over here."

"What are you doing?" asked Francesca, who now stood by the stove and stared up at Rizzy with a strand of spaghetti hanging from the bridge of her nose.

"Nothing, Francesca. Go sit down and stop playing with your food. Cal, come here." Rizzy loosened the cap and emptied the bottle into the pot. "Have you ever had Texas hot sauce?"

Calman shook his head. "Are you sure you're supposed to be doing that?"

"Absolutely. The recipe needs a little kick. Here." She carefully dipped a spoon into the saucy meatballs. "Try it."

Calman swallowed a mouthful and, within seconds, felt his face swell with moisture. His eyes teared, his nose ran, his mouth burned, his ears clogged, and his skin felt ready to explode. He ran to the faucet and stuck his tongue under the flow of cold water. Francesca and her brothers laughed at Calman's performance.

"Just a little something to spice things up tonight." Rizzy rinsed the spoon, hid the empty bottle in a garbage bag under the sink, and was in the midst of washing a few dirty dishes when Lily walked into the kitchen.

"Okay, children, let's get you upstairs and ready for bed. Rosalita, go make sure the table is set properly, will you?"

"Mama, guess what Rizzy just—"

"Francesca, I said upstairs. Hurry now."

Lily had dimmed the overhead lights in the dining room to accentuate the burning heart-shaped candle at the center of the table, a heart that might have been meant to breathe life into the party but was instead mimicking the collective mood by melting and dripping red wax like tears onto a white lace doily. Calman traced the air as it slid visibly past the tiny flame and disappeared into the near darkness above the clenched knuckles of those in prayer.

"Bless us, O Lord, and these thy gifts which we are about to receive from thy bounty." Lily's voice trickled into her cleavage. Calman tried earnestly to hear her, to see her at the end of the table in the flickering light. He could just make out the tiny gold cross around her neck, which blinked like a beacon when she turned toward the light and sighed. He could see her wrists, too, which seemed like soft cushions over deeply embedded bones, unlike Oscar's, whose wrist bones poked at his skin's surface like a wire frame under thin papier-mâché.

Calman could hear Mrs. Blenke and Simon on either side

of him breathing through partially clogged nasal passages. He could feel warmth from their bodies. With his head down in prayer he could see the cloth napkin across Mrs. Blenke's red dress, the gold buckle of Simon's leather belt at the base of his belly, her sideways-crooked fingers, the dry patches on his elbows.

". . . In the name of the Father, the Son, and the Holy Ghost. Amen." Lily raised her head and shifted her silverware in perpendicular fashion to the edge of the table. As if instinctively, she turned toward Rizzy on her right to correct any misbehavior that might have erupted while heads were lowered. Rizzy, indeed, had her white salad bowl atop her head and her knife, spoon, and dinner and dessert forks implanted in her pigtails so they stuck up like sharp horns.

"Rosalita," said Lily, like lava bubbling to the surface. Everyone turned to look at Rizzy.

"Well, nobody'll be patting you on the head tonight," said Mrs. Blenke, smiling at Rizzy.

"I'd say you're ready to take on Carmen Miranda's big ol' fruit baskets, eh?" Simon stole a quick wink at Mrs. Blenke, who seemed to be enjoying his sense of humor.

"It's Attila the Hun," said Oscar.

"Yes, adorable, isn't she?" said Lily. "Such a little devil."

Rizzy beamed at a seething Lily with self-adulation before she dismantled her creation.

"Now, don't you go anywhere," Lily said to her guests. "I'll be right back with the main course."

"The main course?" asked Simon. "Isn't there a salad or something we should be having?"

"Salad comes after the meal; and you'd know that if you paid any attention to the proper way they do things over in Europe." She adjusted a crystal bowl on a corner hutch on her way out. The bowl was filled to the rim with Mary Janes and butterscotch lozenges. "Besides, it's good for the digestion, they say," she sang from the kitchen.

Bob raised his wineglass to examine its edges for chips. He squinted with a scrunched-up nose and twirled the stem in his fingers. "Can't see a blasted thing in here."

"Allow me." Tank's chair scraped the hardwood floor and nearly tipped backward as he stood to turn up the lights. "Bet you didn't even know roll-it-up-a-notch that I put a special dimmer on this here light switch. Told my boys roll-it-up-a-notch, I said now the Dicksons, they ain't no on-and-off types. Need some choices in the matter. You can't skimp on the electrical, nor the plumbing neither. Worst nightmare roll-it-up-a-notch to have your toilet back up and overflow onto the floor and no lights to see what you're stepping into. Now, watch this." The chandelier burst with brightness, like the sun through the exit door after a matinee. Calman blinked and saw spots.

"For crying out loud, Tank, turn it down," said Simon.

"You want to hear about a worst nightmare?" said Bob, staring indignantly at Tank.

Simon emitted a chuckle. "Some real ill will between these

two on account of this house," he explained to Mrs. Blenke and Oscar. "We hired Tank to build it . . . well, now, how long ago was that?"

"Going on seven years," offered Tank. "Remember it roll-it-up-a-notch clear as day." He leaned over to Mrs. Blenke. "First day out, I had the misfortune of stepping on the sharp edge of a saw. Laid up roll-it-up-a-notch all summer. Kept my boys on the job, though, and they did just fine, I'd say. Came down roll-it-up-a-notch on the labor costs, too . . . the Dicksons being good friends and all and me being not quite up to snuff."

"Funny how you always forget to mention the free medical attention," said Bob.

Tank smiled sheepishly. "Had a little problem with the insurance," he said, shifting in his seat. "Dr. Dickson roll-it-up-a-notch, he's a good fix-it man."

"So where did you use to live?" asked Oscar.

"On the other side of town, by the hospital's rehabilitation clinic."

"The one that looks like a college dorm? I always wondered what that was."

"It's a trauma center, people with phantom limbs, sensory loss, psychoses, that sort of thing," explained Bob. "Lily forbids the children to go anywhere near it, Lord knows why. We lived down the street. Small house, no lawn to mow. My idea of comfort."

Rizzy and Calman exchanged glances.

"Why did you move?"

"It was Lily's idea really. She wanted a bigger house and a 'decent neighborhood,' she said."

"I've owned this here land for twenty years," said Simon.

"Why didn't you ever build on it before?" asked Mrs. Blenke.

"Fear of permanency, I suppose. My ma always used to say, 'No one should have his feet rooted to the ground so deep he can't jump for joy.' Mobile homes were always my thing, I guess. People get sick and tired of houses and leave them boarded up and littering the town like junk on the side of the road. Crying shame, if you ask me."

"But you agreed to this house," said Mrs. Blenke.

"I'll tell you something. When Lily gets an idea in her head, there's no stopping her. It's a frightening spectacle, isn't that right, Bobby? She just plum wore me down. Oh, it's good land, really, and I suppose having family around ain't as bad as I thought it'd be." He winked at Rizzy. Rizzy smiled.

Calman had never lived in anything but a city apartment. For the second time that week he wondered what it would be like to live in a house, if it would be big and scary if it was empty.

"I love my wife, but she can get crazy sometimes. You should have seen the first few diagrams she drew up when we decided to build," said Bob. "You could hardly make heads or tails out of them, what with her scribbled arrows and circles and stars for when she thought she was really being clever."

"Remember the widow's walk?" asked Simon. "She drew

these tall columns, like from a Greek temple or something, and a widow's walk at the top."

"What's a widow's walk?" asked Rizzy.

"It's like a deck on the top of a house, usually found on homes along the coastline," explained Bob. "In the old days, women would stand up there and search for their long-lost husbands out at sea. Not much use for them in a desert."

"Mrs. Dickson used to come skipping in roll-it-up-a-notch when we were building, pregnant and all, I remember," said Tank. "She used to twirl roll-it-up-a-notch around the beams like what's his name, the one sings in the rain."

"Gene Kelly," said Oscar.

"She had no idea what a disaster it was turning out to be," said Bob, looking at Tank. "If Lily had had her way, this would have been the Tara of Walla Walla. In the end, it was all sweat and splinters and wasted money. The dining room floor is slanted, the doorways are too short, and that stairway is just completely wrong." He pointed toward the kitchen. "That was one thing Lily was adamant about. She wanted a large sweeping stairway, you know, the kind that's narrow at the top and widens as it curves down toward the dining room. She was going to make the railing this majestic oak, the kind that looks good wrapped with tinsel during the holidays. I think Lily envisioned these grand entrances typical of debutantes or prom queens."

"Yeah, instead the steps dump her directly into the kitchen, where she spends most of her time," said Simon. "The best, though, was Lily in the delivery room when she was giving birth to Fabio, just before the house was finished. Forty some-odd hours of labor, and all the woman could think about was walk-in closets. So much for the miracle of birth."

"Dad," said Lily as she entered the room with a large pot and two bright yellow sunflowery pot holders. "What are you all talking about?"

"Nothing, Lily. Just small talk."

"That's nice. Robert, help me here, will you? Now, I sure don't mean to brag," she said as she began serving the meatballs and accompanying noodles, "but the judges at our local fair here in Walla Walla have always taken a liking to my Swedish meatballs, haven't they, Robert? They won three years in a row, thanks to a very special secret recipe from my mother's side of the family. Please, don't wait for me, I'm on a diet myself, but you all . . . please . . . enjoy." She clapped her hands.

And there it was: the moment, the turning point, as Calman would remember it, when the evening took off like a runaway train. The clap was like a rip in the time/space continuum. It set off cuckoo clocks, teakettles, game-show buzzers, and gongs. It turned floors into ceilings, hands into feet, laughs into snorts, composure into chaos, dinner party into jamboree. Lily's award-winning—and, unbeknownst to her, five-alarm—meatballs were huge wrecking balls swinging into fragile sky-scrapers of playing cards with individual pictures on them of Simon, Mrs. Blenke, all of them as kings, queens, jokers belching, hiccuping, leaning on each other and lamenting life's catch-22's.

Or so it seemed to Calman, who at the moment of the clap took the first sip of his Shirley Temple, mixed by Mrs. Blenke and secretly spiked with peach schnapps by Rizzy, and found it so mm-mm, so smooth and mm-mm, that his sips increased in regularity until he lost count of his sips—for, under these uneasy circumstances, he felt it calming to count something—and then he lost count of his refills.

He was not alone in this endeavor. Like the gunshot that starts the race, Lily's clap prompted her guests to salute with raised forks, and bite chew swallow cough gag gulp their drinks and push away their plates of Lily's award-winning meatballs. Lily saw this and asked politely what was wrong. Simon, not so politely, asked if she was trying to kill them.

"I don't understand," she said, tasting one for herself and then abruptly spitting it out. "Rosalita!" she screamed.

"What? I didn't do anything," said Rizzy.

"Robert, do something. She ruined my meatballs!" Lily was turning red.

"I don't know what she's talking about," Rizzy said to her father.

"Hoo-wee. You're going to get it this time, kid," said Simon, laughing.

"Just calm down, Lily. Rizzy, we'll talk about this later. Lily, why don't we just serve the salad now, all right?"

"I don't see what the problem is," said Tank with a mouthful. "I think they're delicious, Mrs. Dickson."

Lily stormed out in a huff. Her guests had their salads and side dishes and strawberry dessert, but mostly they drank. Before long, they were spitting out the hard consonants and slurring the soft consonants. Oscar's rigid and vertical torso was now arched and limp over the back of his chair; Simon's beard and Tank's cheeks were speckled with sauce; Mr. Dickson practiced Hambones on a set of spoons; and Mrs. Blenke, when she wasn't playing bartender, kept listing toward Calman, so that he had to push her back the other way every now and again.

"I used to bartend at ol' Jenkins's Tavern when we lived in Chicago," said Mrs. Blenke, swaying a raised glass. "Best one in town, if you ask me."

This shocked Calman, for bartenders, he thought, were beefy, muscular men with cigars and five-o'clock shadows who wiped the insides of shot glasses with dirty rags and threw the drunks out after closing. Bartenders didn't smell like rose hand cream.

"She does serve up some mean spirits," said Oscar with a sly grin.

"Oh, be quiet, Oscar. He hated the barroom ever since he was a boy. The regulars used to swing him by his ankles over the pool tables."

"Charming group," said Oscar.

"You lived in Chicago?" asked Simon. "Never been myself. Would love to go."

"Well, let's go," said Mrs. Blenke. "You and me, bub. We'll paint the town red." She and Simon giggled.

Mrs. Blenke took orders and poured, mixed, and had Rizzy carry each drink to the table. Rizzy spiked Calman's Shirley Temple every time. He would follow the swirl of the ice cubes in his glass as she put it in front of him and let the effects of its nectar defeat his anxieties.

Throughout the evening, there was talk at the table as discardable as junk mail: slice it open—*Did you know? Why, isn't it odd that . . . ? How come no one cares that . . . ?*; and throw it out—*No, we didn't . . . no, it isn't . . . because it's easier not to.* The conversations were FYIs and time-passers and innocuous ventings. The Seahawks' season, the governor's agenda, the hereditary nature of bunions. Girdles for men, IQs of chimps, Starbucks on Mars, the Goodyear Blimp. Death by terrorists, death by meteor, death by tsetse fly, death by ennui. Criminals' rights, men in tights. Dot com, dot com, dot com com com. Software, hardware, everywhere a scare there, now everyone's up in arms, may I, may I go.

If this dinner party had been back in Boston, Calman would have excused himself and headed for the TV room. He didn't much care for dinner parties. Usually, his parents didn't invite him to their adult gatherings, except to show him off like a possession. When he was younger, they'd do a nightly routine

183

in front of their guests with exaggerated gestures: they'd pat his tush, calling attention to how cute it was, tell him to put on his PJs and get ready for bed and don't forget to brush, give Daddy a kiss and give Mr. and Mrs. Applebaum a hug, that's it, what a good boy, sweet dreams, pumpkin, doll, love of our life, whoever you are.

On those rare occasions when he did join them, when his grandmother was in town, for example, he got bored quickly. Dinner conversations were bees buzzing around his ears, and he had formed the habit long ago of humming a tune to tune out. *Eat your peas, Calman. You're not eating your peas.* Twenty-one peas on the plate, on the plate. *Vat, you don't like your peas? Peas make you big and strong. Listen to Grandma, she knows. Eat.* Twenty peas on the plate on the plate, twenty peas on the plate. *Look at the prince. Vat, you're too goot for ze peas? One at a time he eats. Ve should all be so important.* If one of those peas should happen to fall . . . *Mother, enough! My son has enough to worry about without your constant nagging* . . . it'll roll right down the hall, the hall.

But here, just when Calman found himself starting to tune out, the conversation would get heated and interesting until Lily broke it off.

"Did I ever tell you about Edna?" Robert was saying. "Edna was the cadaver in my gross-anatomy class first year of medical school. She was sixty-eight, big-boned, and well . . . pale, immobile, and extremely malodorous."

"Malodorous?" asked Mrs. Blenke.

"She stank, Mother," said Oscar.

"Ahem," Lily chimed in. "Here's an interesting fact I just read this morning, everyone." Lily stood with her palms together as if she were preparing to lead a congregation in song. "Did you know that there are approximately six thousand Cheerios in an average fifteen-ounce box? Now, how do you suppose they fit so many in there?"

A pause followed Lily's question. Rizzy was the first to start laughing, followed by Calman, whose laugh barked out like a belch, and then the rest joined in until the room roared with effusive hilarity and Calman, now laughing the loudest, took off his glasses, wiped tears from his eyes, and thought this might just be the most fun he'd ever had. And suddenly he got very tired.

Calman lay on the couch in the living room with one foot hanging off the edge and his mouth as wide open as a chick's waiting for the chewed worm in its mother's beak. He could feel that his mouth was open but he couldn't close it. He could feel that his fingers were fanned out on his chest but he couldn't close them either. Alcohol-induced sleep is a weighted sleep, gravity times ten. It filled his body with lead but his mind with helium. For a moment his eyelids flickered in defiance, and he saw a cobweb on the ceiling. He heard snoring. He had hazy recollections of Simon's banjo and Bob and Oscar's dancing feet and Mrs. Blenke's clapping and the room itself spinning. He remembered thinking the singing, dancing, and clapping were *causing* the room to spin, revving it up like an engine. He couldn't tell how or how long ago he got from the table to the couch and passed out, or what time it was, or where everyone had gone.

"Calman, get up. Jesus, I'd think you were dead if you weren't sawing a log with that snout of yours." Rizzy was standing over him and shaking his shoulder. He experienced a sense of déjà vu from the first time he'd fainted in her room and woken to the sight of her nostrils. This time she was pinching her nostrils shut. "Man. You been farting for the last hour? You sure can make a whole lot of stink."

Calman sat up slowly, painfully. He readjusted his extremities to their natural positions. "Where's my Pepto-Bismol?" he whispered. In all his life he'd never needed it more than he did now. "I don't feel too well."

"I got news for you. You're still drunk, pal. You're slurring your words."

Calman adjusted his glasses and tried to focus on the room, on the clock across the room with the annoying chimes, and on Rizzy. "Why do you have panty hose on your head?"

"I've been robbing banks. Look, just get up. I need your help." She pushed Calman to stand.

"I can't. I think I'm paralyzed."

"Just shut up and work with me here." She gave him another minute of sitting before she yanked his hand and pulled him toward the front door.

"Where are we going?"

"Out."

"What time is it?"

"Almost midnight. You've only been asleep for an hour."

"Did everyone leave?"

"No, they're having a big orgy upstairs." She pulled Calman outside and around to the back of the house.

He was sluggish, still groggy with sleep. He felt the hot summer air of rural America, passive-aggressive in its stillness, its silence. They stood flat against the cool brick wall, inches from a moth-encircled lightbulb. He scraped gravel around with his shoe. He looked at the bulb and then got dizzy from the spots he saw when he blinked. He could hear himself breathe. The darkness out in the onion field sounded like crickets. "I want to go back to sleep," he said. His head was pounding. His body felt shaky.

"Yeah, you told me already. Listen, you have the whole day tomorrow to sleep on the plane, so shut up." She took the panty hose off her head. Her hair, no longer in pigtails, swung in around her neck. "Besides," she said, "this is your last night. We should send you off with a *bang*." The way she said "bang" made Calman take notice of her. He detected a slight drawl of sarcasm or mischief or both. When he looked at her, she changed her stance to manipulate his gaze. She stood tall and erect against the wall so that the most protuberant part of her body was her breasts, bulbous and braless beneath a tight white cotton shirt.

It was the first time Calman had noticed her breasts. All

along she must have been flattening them with sports bras or something and covering them with oversized shirts and overalls, but now they were soft and round and at just about eye level. He couldn't take his eyes off them. They were loose and free and inflating slightly with each breath she took. She was letting him look, too. She was watching him. They were both breathing heavily.

"Give me your hand, big boy," she whispered and she took his outstretched fingers and placed them on her left breast. He closed his eyes and groaned. "Open your eyes," she instructed him. He opened them reluctantly and to his horror found an even more shocking vision than his own hand on the mound of a female breast. Against the white of her shirt, his fingernails glowed a bright red.

He jerked his hand away. "Ew, get it off!" He shook his hands as if they were on fire. He rubbed his fingers hard against his shorts and still the polish shone red. He scraped his nails with his teeth and chipped a few, leaving foul-tasting bits on his lips, like drops of blood or lipstick to match. It was his mother again, right there with her clawing nails the color of blood, a birthmark passed down through the generations. In his blurred state it seemed his hands had become her hands, because his hands were somewhere they weren't supposed to be and her voice rang in his ear, *For God's sake, Calman, don't touch. Keep your hands to yourself. What do we send you to therapy for, can you tell me that, Calman? All that money for nothing.* He heard Rizzy giggle. "Did you do this to me when I was sleeping?" he said, but Rizzy didn't answer. Instead, she jiggled her breasts inches from his face, and then darted off into the night.

He was alone against the wall, looking out into the darkness.

"*Rizzy*," he whispered, a relative scream in the silent night, but only the crickets answered. Had he been sober, he might have gone back inside the house. Had he been himself, he would have crept along the wall back to the couch and curled into a fetal position. How far had Rizzy gone? Was she watching him? He couldn't go back inside, for every boy who ever challenged his bravado was there with him, against the brick wall, pointing at his fingernails and laughing, exacerbating his headache. Overhead was his therapist in a ring of smoke singing *Fight or flight, fight or flight, Calman,* and somewhere out there far beyond the field, without the benefit of a wall to hold him up, was James Bond, 007, champion in the face of fear, a man among men, having himself an adventure and surviving.

Tired and shaky, Calman walked into the darkness, that great equalizer of all things tangible and intangible, where the absence of matter is the matter at hand. *Is anyone out there?* he said, but now his voice sounded invasive and foreign and his breath through his deviated septum sounded like a boiling teapot. The darkness filled in the space behind him and perhaps the spaces in him, for he felt as porous as a ghost. He breathed silently through his mouth and tiptoed toward the onion field. There was little difference between what he saw with his eyes open and what he saw with them closed. As a seasick shipmate looks to the horizon, Calman kept his head turned upward to the flickers of starlight and thought again about God. He thought maybe this time, for the first time, he could feel God's presence instead of trying to see or hear it. But that didn't make sense, for what exactly he was feeling he couldn't say. He only knew what he wasn't feeling: panic. How strange. Of all the times not to experience it. It had become so familiar to him that it was the one thing he could rely on, but now it had abandoned him, bullied off by inebriation. And another thing: he was humming. He didn't remember ever doing that before, except at the dinner table when his grandmother was over. He was humming a song he'd heard Simon singing:

> *My bunny lies over the ocean*
> *My bunny lies over the sea*
> *My bunny lies over the ocean*
> *Oh, bring back my bunny to me*

He imagined a large rabbit stretched over a body of water, who can't move because if he lets go of either landmass, he'll fall and drown. He imagined a boy who threw his bunny over the water and now feels sorry about that. It didn't quite make sense, but the important thing was that Simon's voice was in his head instead of his mother's or his therapist's, and somehow that felt like a step forward.

And so he stepped forward blindly into a dream, looking up to the stars and reaching out with his arms, understanding a kind of freedom he had never experienced before. You trust.

And you go. How simple the formula. In the dark, we are animals connected to our monocelled ancestors who knew nothing more than to change direction when they bumped into barriers.

"*Ow!*" Calman yelled, for he'd stepped on something and it had smacked him in the forehead and knocked him to the ground. Next to his arm, it felt cold and metallic. After further tactile inspection, Calman understood he had stepped on the scoop edge of a shovel and had popped it up. He rubbed his bruised forehead.

"Who's there?" someone said, sending panic back to Calman's world. It was a man's voice, husky and labored.

"I said roll-it-up-a-notch, who's there?"

Calman didn't answer. He didn't move. By now his eyes had begun to adjust to the dark, and if he squinted and tensed his neck muscles, he could just make out Tank's silhouette about five yards away. His heart was pounding. Tank was standing teeteringly with his arms in a downward V.

"Can't take a piss roll-it-up-a-notch in private no more." Tank belched and sighed. Calman heard the steady stream of his urine as it hit the dirt.

And then a scream blitzed the silent dreamy panic-free womb of God-infused nighttime bliss, a scream so loud and high-pitched it made a dog howl, and at the same time, fast, so fast it was like a shooting star, Calman saw Rizzy jump onto Tank's back, crippling his coordination so he fell to the ground like a shot elephant, first to his knees, then to his hands, and onto his side, gasping for air and trying to speak, gasping with his lungs and not just his throat and mouth, and Rizzy, having jumped off just before he rolled flat onto his back, stood triumphant over her prey and said, "Gotcha."

Now no one moved. Even the crickets seemed to have been shocked and awed into silence. Calman had screamed when Rizzy screamed, and his voice still echoed in his ears. He was shaking. His old friends panic and shame were back with a vengeance, lodged in his gut and threatening dry heaves.

"Cal, can you come here?" Rizzy was still standing over Tank.

Calman held his breath.

"Look, I know you're there."

He waited a moment before he said something. "That wasn't funny, you know."

"Just get over here."

Calman crawled to where she stood over Tank.

"He's not moving."

"Well, you scared him."

"I scared you, too, idiot, and you're still crawling. Check and see if he's breathing."

"No, you. You're the one who did it."

Rizzy bent down and brought her ear close to Tank's mouth. "I think he's dead."

They heard faraway laughter. They looked behind them at the house in the distance. Someone yodeled from a doorway.

Rizzy poked Tank's shoulder with her foot, then stepped backward. "Let's get out of here," she said, sounding panicked.

"Wait," he heard himself say. This was too much to process. Death was too much to process in the dark, in a field, three thousand miles away from home, and when there was too much to process, your mind focused on one detail and that detail for Calman was Tank's penis, for he stared at Tank and all he could think about was how they'd find Tank tomorrow, a poor man on his back who'd been taking a piss and had fallen spread-eagled in the dirt with his pants open and his penis exposed for all to see and point at, and in his obituary they'd say just that, and no one, not even a fat man with a speech impediment, should endure that humiliation, so Calman did something no one who knew him would ever have thought he would do: he zipped Tank's pants shut.

"Now your fingerprints are on him."

It didn't matter. Nothing was real but the hard ground. He felt small and insignificant, a particle of dust clinging to the spinning earth, and one day when the earth spins faster and faster out of control and flings everyone and everything off into the darkness, he would hang on. It was his game now, his rules, and while normal people will let go and reach for God in the sky, he will keep his palms to the ground, dig his fingers into the dirt, and grow roots and survive.

A dog barked. "Let's just get out of here, okay?"

Calman was frozen on all fours.

"You can't stay there. We have to get out of here."

He knew that in the end. He followed her through the night, through a dream, through a wicked and warped adventure to the station wagon parked in the driveway of the Dickson home. They climbed into the back, hid under piles of winter clothes, and fell asleep. At some point, the front door of Simon's trailer squeaked open and shut and woke them up. Simon McCory and Eleanor Blenke hooted and hollered their way into the front seat of the station wagon, turned on the engine, and pulled out of the driveway.

"Hoo-wee," yelled Simon as he gunned the engine.

Calman imagined the headlines: *Man Found Dead in Field. Boy and Girl Suspected. Boy and Girl Kidnapped. Boy and Girl Forgotten.*

Calman started to sit up.

"Get down, they'll see you," whispered Rizzy.

Calman eased back down. "Where are we going?" he said weakly. "What if we're going to Chicago, like they said? I'll miss my flight home."

"Would that be so bad?"

There were no more answers and too many questions. In the wake of a burdened past, at the brink of an uncertain future, Calman closed his eyes and let the car wheels roll him back to sleep.

I've Looked at Clouds from Both Sides Now

Out of the left corner of Calman's quarter-moon mouth dribbled the drool of a long night, dampening the bunched flannel shirt he had found for a pillow. Even before he opened his eyes he felt the wet chill and the pinch of the shirt's buttons on his cheek. His neck was cramped; his foot was asleep. He tasted paste, he smelled the regurgitated breath of a thousand old men with bad teeth. He smelled wet dog fur. He smelled rain and gasoline. He saw everything in shades of gray. He thought maybe he was camping in the woods under a wet canvas tent. He heard the steady squeak of windshield wipers. He was being rocked in the cradle, rocked to the rhythms of an engine, a little one that could, a little one that thanked him for helping with getting up the mountain and encouraged him to take heed and find his own energy source and, in a voice that suddenly turned as ironic and as deep as his therapist's voice, instructed him to stop dreaming and wake up.

When he stretched open his eyelids against the crust that had sealed them shut overnight, he observed with a vague recollection of previous events that he was in the back of a moving station wagon. His body was enveloped in mildewy clothes in large masculine sizes and sturdy stock, the clothes of beefy lumbermen, he imagined, with names like Joe Henry or John Bull, but most likely owned by Simon McCory, who, if Calman remembered correctly, was probably the one driving the station wagon. Rain trickled diagonally down the back windows. It felt like early morning.

It took Calman a few minutes to confirm that his current situation, as bizarre as all the fictional ones he had dreamed up, was in fact the real one. He yawned and blinked hard and rotated his eyeballs in their sockets before he patted around for his glasses and placed them back on his face. Calman was now in the habit of putting his glasses on before he did anything else, but it hadn't always been that way. Rather, he had had a different habit—of losing his glasses and just about puncturing himself to death while searching for them in a blur amid the various sharp edges in his bedroom (and sometimes fainting as a result). At certain times, he would collect all the towels in the apartment to cover desk corners, doorknobs, and other jutting objects in his room poised to take advantage of his carelessness, until his mother said *enough already with the towels* and bought him a night table on which to place his glasses and have them handy first thing in the morning. His glasses felt misshapen and odd now, but they fine-tuned the vision of Rizzy asleep next to him.

He turned to her as slowly as he could so as not to rustle anything that would wake her. She lay on her side, facing him, tucked into a frayed and filthy beach towel. Her brown hair was spread out across her own makeshift duffel-bag pillow. She had sweetly sour breath that was faintly audible as tiny puffs of air brushed past her soft nose hairs and the small ball of snot in her right nostril. Calman thought he might like her best when she was sleeping. There was a seemingly infinite amount of time to study her without an explosion of consequences or regret. He hadn't noticed before how long her lashes were, for example, or that she had wispy baby-hair sideburns. Her cherubic face was slightly swollen and shiny from sleep. Calman felt protective of her. He felt her vulnerability and thought for a moment that he might like to kiss her again.

But then his stomach began gurgling like a water cooler, loud enough that Calman was worried it might wake her up. He remembered having a substantial amount of liquor, maybe more than he'd had at his own bar mitzvah when his great-uncle, before the Torah reading, kept handing him flasks filled with Slippery Nipples *because Hebrew, as it is said, is best understood with drunken slurs, don't you forget it, boychik*, but even then he didn't feel as ill as he did now. He couldn't tell if he was still drunk, or hungover *as it is said*, for he wasn't sure he could identify the exact feeling of either state. He just knew his temples, *ha ha, good one, boychik,* were throbbing and his stomach, now that he was aware of its condition, was dancing to its own tune.

Rizzy awoke like the fast-forward viewing of a blooming flower, twisting and turning and widening toward the sky. She bunched her covering into the corner of the car, then placed her palm at the bottom edge of the window, perhaps to steady herself and recall where she was and why. Then she turned to Calman, looking up at his hair that had molded with sweat into a standing position atop his head. He patted his hair with little cooperation. Nothing cooperated, not his sweaty hair, not his throbbing head, not his grouchy stomach, not his bright red fingernails, *oh, God, I wasn't dreaming,* not his drumming heart, now pounding the inside of his chest like an angry tenant at the door of a head-banging rock-and-roll neighbor. He felt like his body had separated into parts.

"Where are we?" whispered Rizzy.

"In the back of the car."

"Doh, idiot. Where are we headed? Have you seen any road signs?"

He hadn't, but then he hadn't been looking. Now that he was looking, he couldn't really focus without getting dizzy. Anything he saw snuck up from behind, whizzed past them, shrank into the distance, and eventually disappeared before he could make an identification. What he preferred was to focus on nothing and have everything blur into one steady movement. He'd always liked road trips. As long as he was moving he was okay, because in his mind it was movement toward something, not away from something. And there was this theory: once you were moving it was easier to continue moving. Say, for example, you need to get to an emergency room. If you're in your room, it's a hassle and a half (his mother often added "a half" to emphasize her main points) to pull yourself together, call a cab, and get there. But if you're already in the car, already moving, it's easy enough to keep on going, even if you have to turn around.

Rizzy stole a peek at Simon and Mrs. Blenke in the front seat. "Do they know we're here?"

"I don't think so."

"Good."

Simon and Mrs. Blenke had talked about going to Chicago, and from what he knew of geography, that was halfway back to Boston. Maybe, he thought, he could get a flight from there and make it back in time before his parents noticed he was missing.

"Man, I wish I could get out of these clothes, I feel disgusting," said Rizzy. She smelled her armpit. "I stink, too," she said with a grimace. "And don't look at me like that. You ain't no bed of roses either."

Calman remembered that he had none of his belongings with him, except what he was wearing. They had jumped into the car so quickly, they hadn't thought to pack. Then again, they'd thought they'd still be in the driveway the next morning instead of on some highway going who knows where.

It was a rather disturbing experience not to have his things with him. It was a new kind of aloneness. It was one thing to be far away from your parents, your friends if you had any, and your therapist, but another to be far away from the material possessions that defined you, that protected you in the womb of familiarity. When he had first arrived and had to lug his suitcase up to the house, he had cursed his mother for making him pack so much. But now it was a different story. He needed his neatly balled socks that smelled of fabric softener, his comb with six teeth missing, his lucky bicentennial quarter, his lucky magenta crayon, his lucky kiwi-flavored ChapStick, and his lucky absorbent, flexible, odor-eating right shoe insert. He was out of luck for sure. He even missed the letter from his mother now that it was gone.

Calman felt cut loose without a life vest. So many of the things he chose to keep were good-memory holders and now that they were gone, he couldn't recall with any clarity what had gone right in his past. All he had was what he was wearing. His pants and his sneakers bore no memory for him, but thank God for his shirt. The short-sleeved, gray cotton shirt he wore was plain and simple. His mother had bought it for him at Filenes's downtown, not the basement but the department store where it smelled like glamorous women in magazines, like his mother's friends when they first appeared at the door for dinner parties. The shirt was just a shirt, but on the front, right above his heart, was a year-old brown splotch of Ben & Jerry's Chocolate Fudge Brownie ice cream bought next to the

State House in Boston during a march against overpopulation that he'd gone to with his father. He wasn't sure how he felt about overpopulation when he himself kept wishing for more people in his life, but he was just glad to be with his father when his father was in a good mood, away from his mother.

Ira Pulowitz was affectionate that day. Calman remembered a cupped palm on his shoulder, the touch of an adult hand that wasn't fixing something or tucking something in or wiping something off. His father held his hand on Calman's shoulder to connect, father to son, and he left it there for exactly half a block down State Street, and then said *Hey, let's get some ice cream,* which made Calman feel like the gold medalist in the race for parental adoration. But when he got home, his mother had rolled her eyes at the stain he had made, and had said to his father, *Look at him, you let him walk around like that?* and had grabbed at his shirt to pull it over his head while yelling at his father about being late and lazy and jelly-spined. Out of habit, Calman pointed his arms upward in a standard surrender position while his mother twisted him about and yanked the shirt up over his head, bending the flaps of his ears inward, making his hair fly up in a static frenzy, and twisting his glasses to a 45-degree angle across his face so that he looked like a cartoon character who, after saying, "You wouldn't hit a guy with glasses, would ya?" got punched. She took his pants, too, and left him standing there in the living room in his Carter's underpants as she walked down the hall and threw them in the washing machine to wash them *right this minute* because *God forbid there should be just one minute in the life of Bridgette Pulowitz when something isn't perfect,* his father was yelling as he followed her to the washing machine. As luck would have it, his parents went into their bedroom to continue their argument in private, which gave Calman the opportunity to remove his shirt from the machine before it got wet and hide it for several months to let sink in the remains of the day his father and he were as close as they ever were and would probably ever be again. And after that day, Calman made a habit of staining his clothing when there was an occasion to remember.

"Move over. You're touching me," whispered Rizzy, pushing at his elbow. "I didn't give you permission to touch me."

Calman swung his elbow to the other side of his body and scrunched over to his side of the car, but found it was nearly impossible not to touch Rizzy in such cramped quarters. He felt locked into place and claustrophobic, and now that he really thought about his situation in a fully awakened state, he felt the urge to throw up. If they weren't planning on telling Simon or Mrs. Blenke that they were there, how would they live? How would they be able to go to the bathroom? How would they eat? He had seven dollars and thirty-two cents in his pocket, and priorities being what they were, he'd have to use that to pay for a new bottle of Pepto-Bismol instead of food. Maybe they'd be on the road for months and he'd miss the beginning of school. His parents would eventually give up their search for him and he'd be a stowaway forever, wearing the same shirt and pants and underpants he'd been sweating in for the last twenty-one hours, forty-two minutes, and twelve seconds, thirteen seconds, fourteen seconds.

"I think we should tell your grandfather we're here," he said nervously.

"Forget it. They'll only take us back, and we can't go back. Don't you remember? Or were you too drunk?"

Calman had a blurred memory of seeing Tank on the ground in the dark, exposed and immobile, and of a feeling of utter panic, as if he had something to do with why Tank wasn't moving.

"What's wrong with you? You're hyperventilating. Are you having another episode?"

"I'm just . . . I'm not feeling well."

"Sh. Lower your voice, they'll hear you. You're just hungover. You're fine."

"My stomach is doing somersaults." Calman attempted to sit up and put his head between his legs, but Rizzy grabbed his forearm and pulled him back down.

"Get down. They'll see you."

"A bag," Calman said between deep, quick breaths. "I need to breathe into a bag. I need a bag."

"I don't have one," said Rizzy, patting around where they lay. "All right, just calm down. Watch me. Breathe when I breathe. Come on." Rizzy exaggerated her breathing and coached him the way doctors did on TV for women giving birth.

Calman followed her lead and tried to slow his breathing.

"Look, if it gets really bad for us, we'll tell them we're here, okay?"

"Okay," whispered Calman.

Rizzy slowly repositioned her body to get more of a stretch, and Calman noticed, as she rolled onto her side, that she winced and pressed down with her palm on the lower part of her abdomen. He thought he heard a slight grunt or exhalation of pain.

"Does it hurt?" he whispered, gaining control of his breathing.

"Does what hurt?" Rizzy hid her hands under the towel.

Calman didn't answer, for he figured out that the answer could be that truths sometimes need space and time to emerge.

"Kind of, yeah," she said after a silence.

"Why does it hurt?"

"How should I know?" she said aloud, then turned to the front of the car to see if she had said it too loudly. She lay back down and looked out the window. It was a long stretch of highway they were on. "All I can tell you is it sucks being a girl."

But it's hard to be a boy, too, thought Calman. Would he rather be a girl? What is a girl like anyway? He still hadn't figured that out. He was often accused of being girlish and Rizzy acted more like a boy than he did. And then they had to grow up. Maybe Rizzy was finding it just as hard to become a woman as he was finding it to become a man.

"Is it your period?"

She turned to look at him. "What do you know about that?"

"I know it can be painful sometimes because my mom complains of cramps and things." Calman's stomach was hurting with what felt like half nausea and half sympathy pain. Rizzy turned back around and was silent for a few minutes. Calman suspected she was thinking things through.

"My period last month was a killer," she whispered after a time. "I guess that can happen. And this time it's not any better. In fact, it feels worse because it's like it won't stop. I can't believe a person can lose that much blood."

Calman felt bad for her. He tried to imagine what it would be like to have your body suddenly change like that. "Does it feel like a big change?" he asked. "I mean, were you upset when you got it?"

"Are you kidding? Who in their right mind would want to deal with this girly crap?" Then she softened her voice and sounded sort of wistful. "I was the last girl in my class to get it."

Calman was confused. Was she glad she got it or wasn't she? Did she mind being the last of her peers to get it or was she glad it happened later? Maybe she was confused, too, or maybe she felt both ways.

Up front, Simon cracked open a window and introduced new noise into their mobile cocoon. It had stopped raining out, but everything still felt damp inside. Calman and Rizzy peeked over the backseat, enough to see Simon's tam-o'-shanter askew and Mrs. Blenke's polished toenails resting on the dashboard.

Simon and Mrs. Blenke made Calman think about his grandparents on his father's side. "Did you know your grandmother?" he asked.

"No, she died of cancer when Lily was like eighteen or nineteen. But I've seen pictures. She was perfect. She must have been the prom queen or whatever they had back then. Everybody loved her. My grandfather would have done anything for her, so I heard. But Lily really never talks about her."

Calman thought about mothers of mothers, of mothers of mothers of sons, of what might be explainable that up until now seemed inexplicable. "Maybe your grandmother was as hard for your mom to deal with as your mom is for you."

This time, Rizzy didn't shoot back a response right away or make fun of him for saying "deal with" or some other therapy-speak. Calman was delighted that maybe he had said something that she hadn't thought of before.

"Lily as a teenager," she said finally, thoughtfully. "Now, there's a scary thought." Just then the car slowed down. They were exiting the highway. "Perfect timing. I gotta pee like a racehorse."

The car made a few turns and parked diagonally along what looked like the main street of a small rural town. The street sagged in the middle with brick buildings, benches, bike racks, and other traces of man-made activity, but then stretched up and out on both sides to distant mountains.

"Get down," said Rizzy. She and Calman covered themselves with loose clothing and lay flat and still. Simon and Mrs. Blenke got out of the car and walked around the back. Their voices were muffled and soon inaudible as they made their way to the diner across the street. Rizzy signaled to Calman when it was safe to sit up.

"Can they see us?"

"I don't think so," said Rizzy. "They'll be there for a while. Let's get out of here."

"Out of the car? You think that's a good idea?" Calman had all sorts of scenarios running through his brain, none of them desirable. It seemed too hard to deal with their current situation when he had serious things to think about, like the death of Tank. *Oh, God, was Tank really dead?* Rizzy must be thinking of that, too.

"You can stay here if you want, but I'm getting some fresh air and some food."

"We don't have any money," said Calman, figuring he'd keep his seven dollars and change a secret until they were really desperate.

"So we'll rob a bank."

Was that another truth-lie? It could be, thought Calman. He never knew with Rizzy. He recalled a documentary he'd seen on TV about the outlaws Bonnie and Clyde, about how a life of crime for the couple had led to a life of murder and eventually their early deaths, all bloody and dramatic and sickening.

"So what's with the face?" said Rizzy. "I was just kidding."

"Have you ever stolen anything before?"

"Well, yeah. Of course. It's a rite of passage. They expect it of us. Why, haven't you?"

"No." Which was a truth-lie in itself. A boy he knew had once stolen two grape Popsicles from the neighborhood ice-cream truck. The boy had stood in front of Calman on line, and when the ice-cream man with his apron and crabby disposition went to the front of his truck to turn off the truck's circus tune that could be heard three blocks away *because,* he said, *the music, man, the music plays in my head twenty-four hours a day, man, and makes me want to kill someone, man,* that's when the boy reached in and grabbed two Popsicles, gave one to Calman, and ran off. *Hey, man, what'd you do, what'd I miss?* the ice-cream man had yelled weakly after the boy and then asked Calman, *What just happened, man?* to which Calman stared at him like a deer in headlights and replied *Nothing.* Calman had been wary of the ice-cream man for months because he had a tendency to drive up on sidewalks and knock over garbage cans, and because he kept calling Calman *man,* which to Calman was perhaps one of the most depressing and confusing words in all of history. But why he didn't own up to the Popsicle in his pocket he didn't know. He just bought his own Creamsicle, put it in his other pocket, thanked the ice-cream *man,* and headed toward a nearby park. In the park, the boy had asked for his Popsicle back without even thanking Calman for being an accomplice. Calman remembered sitting on a swing for a long time, thinking about what he had done and how it felt. The clearer memory, though, was when he left the park because it got too hot, and saw his mother sitting out on the stoop, staring at his leg because by then the Creamsicle that he had completely forgotten about had mostly melted and dribbled down his shorts and into his sneakers. *What is that?* she asked. *It's a Creamsicle,* he had said. *You put it in your pocket?* she said, and it was then that he realized that what he had done was the dictionary definition of stupid. What he knew he'd remember most from the whole incident was not that he had helped steal something but rather the look on his mother's face, the Oh-well-there-goes-Harvard look that bored a hole in him the size of a man.

"For now we'll be fine," said Rizzy. "I'm sure there's enough change lying around in this mess for some aspirin." She swung over into the backseat and then the front seat, looking for coins in the glove compartment, in the cup holders, and on the floor. When she had collected a handful of change and scored with a ten-dollar bill from the pocket of Mrs. Blenke's sweater, she opened the car door on the side facing away from the diner. She kept low to the ground. "Are you coming, princess?"

Calman peeked over at the diner. Simon and Mrs. Blenke were at a table by the window, looking at their menus. "Yeah, I'm coming." He followed Rizzy outside, and as he'd been well trained to do most of his life, having grown up in a city, he locked the door.

"Stop! Aw, crap!"

"What? What did I do?"

Rizzy pulled at the door handle and hit the window with her fist. "You just locked us out, idiot. How do you think we're going to get back in without them noticing?"

"Oh, God. I wasn't thinking. What do we do now?" Calman started to panic.

"I don't know. Calm down. Let's just go. We'll figure it out."

Calman followed Rizzy around the car. When the coast was clear, they ran single-file in spurts from car to mailbox, mailbox to Dumpster, Dumpster to truck, truck to the next block where they were finally out of view of the diner and could walk upright. They were also out of eyeshot of the car, a fact that reminded Calman that he needed a drugstore to purchase his Pepto-Bismol.

But nothing seemed to be open. They passed by a post office, a five-and-dime, even a small market with a large advertisement for beef jerky in its window display and a bold CLOSED sign on the door. The basset hound in the doorway of the convenience store didn't even pick up its head when they passed. It followed them with its eyes and then went back to sleep. That was all there was to Main Street, with the exception of the closed bank across the street, which Calman neglected to mention. The trees seemed freeze-framed, the cicadas buzzed in and out with the sounds of electric razors. The stop sign had been killed with bullet wounds, and the sidewalks held secrets. It was a town in a coma.

"So what do we do now?" asked Calman nervously. His agoraphobia was setting in. He didn't see a drugstore, or a supermarket, or even a living person who could, if need be, point him in the direction of the nearest hospital. The air was crisper than it was in Walla Walla, but it was still hot, and if he looked far down Main Street until it converged into a single point, the street turned to liquid oil and spoke to him with the possibility of drowning.

"Stop asking me that." Rizzy took a detour toward a group of bushes up a hill from the street. "Look, I have to pee. Tell me if you see someone coming." She disappeared behind the bushes.

Calman looked around. Nothing. He needed her to be quicker, as he was about to burst. "My turn," he said when she came back.

He stood with his feet apart, waiting to make his mark on wherever it was they were. *God, where are we?* He thought about how far away he was from home. What would his therapist say? Wasn't this both fight and flight? Can one even do both at the same time? And what about his mother? Maybe when she arrived back from her trip and found him missing, she'd call the police and put an ad on a milk carton. Maybe she'd tell newspaper reporters how selfish she was to put her son on a plane to go clear across the country to visit someone he had never met before, just because she needed a vacation in Florida.

Something rustled the leaves to his left and startled him

back to his surroundings. The problem with the ground, he thought, was that there were too many shades of brown and green, too many moving things that looked like nonmoving things, and too many hiding places. This wasn't privacy, this was a convention of creepy crawly spectators and all around him *out there* had to be all things toothy and territorial.

"C'mon," yelled Rizzy. "What's taking you so long? I'm coming up there."

That was all he needed. The feel of the release in the open air, the sound of it hitting leaves, the sight of it trickling down along dirt—this had to be one of the best feelings in the world, he thought. How come he had never peed outside before?

"Look," said Rizzy, pointing his gaze down a side street when he returned. "There's a gas station. Let's check it out."

The gas station was not only open, but stocked with sundry items for travelers. Calman found a bottle of Pepto-Bismol, which he rubbed in his palms like a lucky rabbit's foot. Down the aisle he also found a bottle of nail polish remover, but he was dismayed at the price. He couldn't afford both bottles, and now he didn't know which to buy. Should he save his stomach or his manhood?

Rizzy had made a collection of two candy bars, a can of soda, tampons, and a bottle of Tylenol Extra Strength Caplets and had plopped them down on the counter in front of several unappetizing bakery goods wrapped in cellophane. Calman was repulsed by anything in plastic wrap. The frosting on the Dan-ish was mashed down, the muffins were misshapen, the sandwiches looked like they had been suffocated to death. Maybe they were healthier than the name-brand products that had been prepackaged, machine-processed, and chemically preserved to outlast earth itself, but they didn't have any lists of ingredients or expiration dates or warnings of side effects or cute television commercials and catchy jingles like Nabisco did, for example, to make you feel warm and fuzzy inside. This was not comfort food, it was *dis*comfort food, and Calman found he couldn't even look at it without feeling nauseous.

The shirtless cashier checked out Rizzy from head to waist and up again, and smiled. "Hey," he said to her, flexing his puffed-out, oil-stained pecs. He looked alarmingly like the ice-cream man from Calman's criminal past, only he wore a bandanna on his head and had a ring through his nipple. Calman couldn't help staring at his bare chest as he rang them up.

"You," he said, looking at Calman, ready, no doubt, to poke fun, find fault, or pick a fight. "Stop looking at my tits." He stood tall, mashed his breasts together, and fluttered his eyelashes with mock femininity. "Can't you see me for who I am, and not just as a sex symbol? You boys are all alike." He laughed at his own antics.

Rizzy laughed, too, in an exceedingly annoying way Calman hadn't heard before. She ran her fingers through her hair and asked for a pack of cigarettes.

"But you don't smoke," said Calman, which prompted a death look from Rizzy and another chuckle from Nipple Boy.

"My brother's an idiot. Ignore him."

Her brother? Calman watched the two of them entwine their goopy gazes and giggles until he couldn't take it anymore. This tattooed teenager with the dopiest grin Calman had ever seen was leaning toward her over the counter, shifting his weight from foot to foot like a lion about to pounce, making her smile coquettishly and causing her to have tunnel vision. And Rizzy was all of a sudden frighteningly feminine, the way she stood with one foot crossed over the other, head tilted, her neck exposed, her eyelashes aflutter. *What was going on?* Calman felt like pulling on her sleeve and screaming, *This guy is the idiot! Let's get out of here,* but the aura around their bodies felt like an energy field that would zap him to his death if he reached out to touch it. Plus, he didn't want to take his hands out of his pockets for fear the cashier would see his red fingernails. He couldn't risk the embarrassment of buying nail polish remover from this guy either, and Rizzy wasn't offering any help at the moment. He was contemplating stealing the bottle.

"How much for this stuff?" he said in an impotent voice to a boarded-up world. He was the wolf, trying to blow down a brick house. "Um," he said again, clearing his throat, "how much for this stuff?" But Rizzy was gone, she wasn't *his* at this moment, whatever word should follow "his"—friend, girl-friend, pen pal, partner in crime. She had kicked him into the pit of idiot-sibling status and that was, well . . . that was just unacceptable. *Tell them how you feel, Calman. Tell them you're angry. Tell them you're hurt. Tell them you're* "angry! Very very angry!" he blurted out before he could stop himself.

It was a gunshot in Pleasantville. Rizzy and her new boy-friend turned to him with queer stares and awaited an explanation.

"What I mean is, I'm feeling a bit ignored and I think if you can just tell us how much we owe you we can get out of your way and get going to where we're supposed to be going, because I should tell you we're kind of in a hurry." They sounded like someone else's words, someone else's voice. What he had just said felt like a belch, an unexpected bodily outburst that he should perhaps apologize for and blame on his hangover. Just seconds after he spoke, he couldn't remember what he had said. He had a vague sense that the lasso he had tossed out to encircle his meaning had fallen short of its elusive target and landed in a limp pile on the ground.

"God, Cal," said Rizzy. "Get you."

The cashier laughed out loud. "What a pansy."

"Leave him alone," said Rizzy. "Here. How much do we owe you?"

It worked. Whatever he'd said seemed to cause a tremor in the spell she was under.

The cashier smiled slyly and rang up the items on the counter, one by one. "One Sprite. One Kit Kat. One Milky Way. One bottle of Tylenol. One box of tampons for the pretty lady. And one bottle of pretty pink liquid for Mr. Sensitivity."

"Just tell us how much it is," said Rizzy, not quite back to her old self, but defensive, at least, on Calman's behalf.

"That's $13.89."

Rizzy counted her change on the counter. "Where are we, anyway?" she said.

"Okanogan County. You're about an hour south of the border."

"The border of what?"

"Canada, babycakes. How come you don't know where you are? You have amnesia or something?"

Both Rizzy and Calman's mouths hung open; they stared at the cashier, then turned to each other.

"Simon must have gone north," said Rizzy, branching off into a near-private side conversation with Calman.

"But I thought they were going to Chicago. I heard them say last night that they wanted to go to Chicago."

"Well, obviously they changed their minds. Or they're taking the long way around. Hell, we could be heading for the North Pole, for all I know. Simon would do that."

"Who's Simon? Your boyfriend?" the cashier said to Rizzy as he reached out to stroke her hair.

"Don't touch me."

"Oh, now suddenly you're icy cold." The cashier didn't stop. He touched her hair again, and when she reached up to swat away his hand, he caught her wrist and pulled her toward him over the counter.

As he had done during the Roland Gates incident in the parking lot of the church, only now with all the confidence one gains when one has nothing more to lose, Calman entered the battle. He grabbed the can of Sprite from the bag and lobbed it full force at the cashier's head. The cashier fell backward and cried out in pain.

Rizzy quickly grabbed the bag of goods. "Run," she yelled. "Let's get out of here!"

Calman took one step toward the door and stopped abruptly. He ran back to the aisle with the nail polish remover, grabbed a bottle, and then bolted out the door as fast as he could. He ran to keep up with Rizzy, but all he kept thinking about was that he was almost in Canada and that he had never been to Canada and that in all likelihood there was everything to run from but nothing in Canada that he could think of to run *to* and so he stopped running. He had a headache. He slowed to a walk, then he stood bent over with his hands on his knees, and then he sat right where he was, on the side of the road, in a patch of dirt. He didn't want to go any farther in any direction. He just wanted to sit.

Rizzy eventually slowed, too, and made her way back to him. "What are you doing?"

"I'm sitting."

"You're sitting. That's great." Rizzy plopped the bag down at her feet and crossed her arms.

Calman looked up. "You can go on. I'm sitting here. I'm done. My head hurts. My stomach hurts. And it's . . . it's just too much to process anymore."

"Process? Jesus, this is going to be one of your therapy moments, isn't it. Fine." She sat down next to him and waited for Calman to say more, but he didn't. She grabbed the paper bag and took out the Tylenol. "You want some?"

"Is it chewable?"

"You've got to be kidding."

"Never mind," said Calman. He needed to be better about stopping some of the things that burped out of his mouth, he thought. "Yeah, give me some. And the Pepto Bismol." He swallowed the pill, making a pug face, and took a swig of the Pepto Bismol. He accepted the half of the chocolate bar Rizzy handed him, and ate quickly. He poured nail polish remover onto his shirt and began wiping his fingernails clean. New stains, he thought.

Rizzy drew in the dirt with a stick.

"Riz," he said, "I still don't understand what it is about your mom that bugs you so mu—"

"Not again," she interrupted, throwing the stick into the street. "You don't stop. Didn't we just have our big heart-to-heart in the car? Wasn't that enough? Talk, talk, talk, all you ever do is talk. How much of this can you take in one day, for God's sake?"

Welcome to my life, thought Calman. "Okay, sorry. But you still owe me a truth, you know. And I don't know why you're not telling me what's going on, like what happened at that building you showed me next to where you used to live and why you're being so mysterious about stuff. I'm just curious."

"A girl should have a shroud of mystery around her."

"Forget it. Never mind." Calman rubbed his temples. The smell of the nail polish remover was making his headache worse. No cars passed them on the road. No birds flew overhead. The ants were busy by his sneakers, but that was about it. He felt like giving up on everything there was to give up on.

"Okay, so Lily and I don't like each other. Plain and simple. What's wrong with that?"

"That doesn't sound right. She's your mother."

"So what does that mean? What difference does it make? Your family isn't perfect."

"I know. My mother's hard to get along with, too, but I don't know. She's my mother, that's all. I feel bad sometimes because she and my father don't always get along." He paused here and thought about his mother's letter. Quietly he added, "I sometimes think they don't like each other anymore. So I try to be nice."

Again the silence made way for truth, and Rizzy spoke. "Well, my mother, she's crazy for real. I'm sure you've figured that out by now. I mean, when I was little, she used to dress me up like a princess in a frilly dress and show me around. I had to sit with my legs crossed, fold my napkin on my lap, say thank you and please, and never get dirty or do anything sudden. I'm her first daughter, and she must have been waiting a long time for a real live doll. Get this: she used to go into the five-and-dimes and card stores around town and you know those picture frames they'd have on display? When no one was looking she'd take out the fake pictures of the models and put my picture in them. I saw her do it a million times. It was so embarrassing."

"So what happened? What changed?"

"Shut up, I'm getting there. And by the way, it's not like it changed overnight. We don't wise up in a day. But I guess, yeah, it was when Julia died."

"Who's Julia?"

"When I was about eight or nine, I had this friend, Julia, who was also my age and lived at the trauma center I showed you, down the street from where we used to live. I just met her one day and we started talking and I liked her. She was really sarcastic and funny. She was Mexican, too, and I thought that was the coolest thing. She had an awesome accent and great stories. Made me want to go to Mexico. I thought, you know, someday she and I would go and she could show me around. But even though we didn't talk about it I knew something was wrong with her. She was in a wheelchair. It was fun for me at the time. I pushed her around and we did all sorts of tricks with it, laughing till we couldn't breathe. But still, I knew something was wrong.

"Anyway, Lily hated the fact that I spent so much time over there. Of course, Julia being in a wheelchair and being Mexican clearly didn't fit in with her freak fairy tale. So she gets it in her head that I should stop going over to the center, that it wasn't appropriate for me to be seen there. So, of course, I ignored her and went anyway. She gave me hell. I think she was completely shocked that I stood up to her and didn't do what she said, that I could scream at her just as loud as she screamed at me.

220

"This went on for weeks, and then one day she just exploded. We were outside in the yard. She starts yelling, horrible insults about Julia, like about her being a cripple and a foreigner and how I'm better than she is and I should know better than to hang out with her, blah blah blah. We turn around and, the next thing you know, there's Julia on the sidewalk in her wheelchair. I was so horrified. We didn't see her there at first, but I know she heard. I know for a fact she was hurt."

"What'd you do?"

"I could have killed Lily right there, but I just ran away."

"Where did you go?"

"I hid out in Julia's room. My dad knew I was there. He let me stay overnight with her, but then something happened and she got really sick and they wouldn't let me stay in her room anymore. They made me go home and I never saw her again."

"Julia? Why not?"

"She died two weeks later."

"Oh, no, she died?" *Death, too much of it, too much of it.* Calman felt the kind of deep sadness that comes from a slow buildup.

"Yeah. Lily, she got quiet for a while, I guess she felt bad, but she never apologized. Can you believe that? I won't ever forgive her for that."

"I think you were lucky to have a friend like that at all. I never have."

For the first time he saw pity in Rizzy's eyes. And real warmth.

"I haven't told that story to anyone before," she said.

Calman accepted her friendship with a nod and a half smile. It was nice, this. So much flight and fight, but here he was with a friend. His breathing was steady, his glasses were clean, his clothes were stained and dirty, his headache was subsiding. With his palms to the ground, he pushed himself up and stood above her. "Rizzy," he said, "let's go home."

Rizzy looked up at him a few times. She didn't argue. She didn't move. She didn't speak. Then suddenly she grabbed her abdomen and started moaning.

"What? What is it? What's the matter?"

Her moaning was getting louder. "Ow! It hurts. Cal! It hurts!"

"Oh, my God! Can you get up?"

Now she was yelling. "Help me! The pain!" She writhed on the ground.

"Oh, God! Okay, don't move! I'll go get help!"

Now Calman ran. He ran so fast he was scared he would topple over. He ran and ran and ran forever, is how he'd remember the way it felt just before he reached the glass door of the restaurant, saw Mrs. Blenke behind the door, saw the perfect little o shape of her eyes and lips when she saw him, saw her fling the door open and exclaim, "Alvin!", felt the heavy glass door hit him in the forehead and knock him out cold.

Keep on the Sunny Side

"Alvin! Can you hear me, Alvin?"

Calman felt the mist of Mrs. Blenke's breath on his cheeks. When he finally opened his eyes, he was looking directly down her bodice. He had been picked up and moved just inside the diner, and now his head was pressed tightly against Mrs. Blenke's bosom. The bow in the valley of her pink satin bra tickled the tip of his nose. Her tan, baggy skin smelled like tissues.

"Alvin, sweetie. It's Eleanor. Remember me? El-ea-nor." Her makeup was clumped and sporadic in the crevices of her chapped lips and tired eyelids. Her big red fleshy lips looked like they were pressed up against glass. She touched a wet rag to his forehead, which sent a stinging pain straight through to the back of his skull.

"Ow," he yelled, drawing his hand up to his head.

"Now that's just what we wanted to hear, son . . . like a newborn's wailing." Simon bent down toward Calman, resting his nine fingers upon his knees. Strands of gray hair clung to his black T-shirt under his brown leather vest, too small to close over his extended belly. "Looks like you're going to be just fine. Hoo-wee, did you give us a scare. Like seeing a ghost. What in God's name are you doing all the way up here?"

Calman touched his forehead, winced from the pain, then looked at his finger. "Blood," he breathed. "I'm bleeding. I need to go to the hospital . . ." *Hospital. Rizzy.* "Rizzy!" he gasped. "She needs help. She's that way." He moved to get up, but Simon and Mrs. Blenke told him to stay put. He told Simon more specifics about where to find Rizzy. Simon took off to go look for her.

"Now, let's give you some air," said Mrs. Blenke, cradling his shoulders in her lap. "Get your wits about you."

Calman sat up slowly. He felt woozy, but the wet rag on his temples was helping. He told himself he should take deep breaths, but the air in this foreign place felt like it was one element off from the air he was used to, and his lungs were scrambling to make adjustments.

"So how *did* you get here?"

"We were hiding in the back of the car when you took off," Calman explained.

"My heavens, you were quiet as church mice. What happened to Rizzy?"

224

"We were talking and then she was in pain and couldn't walk. I had to run back and get help."

"Well, I'm sure Simon will find her. In the meantime, let's get you washed up, and get you something to eat. You must be starved."

In the men's room of the diner, Calman leaned into the mirror above the sink and examined the bruise on his forehead. The door hit him in the same spot as the shovel had hit him. It hurt, but it was a bruise, and bodily bruises, he was beginning to think, were just about the coolest thing.

He returned to the diner and slid into the booth across from Mrs. Blenke, who was sipping her coffee from a spoon. "Feel better?" she asked. She waved at the steam above her coffee cup, then dropped in an ice cube from her water glass. They were the only patrons in the diner this early. A fat hound dog by the cash register grunted, and shifted positions. The music was too low to decipher, too brassy to ignore.

"Yeah, I guess," he answered lazily. His head was still throbbing, but he felt hungry. He opened the large, frayed plastic menu and knocked over a bottle of hot sauce. The fat hound dog barked once—a weak, laborious, double-chin-swinging bark—and went back to sleep.

As if summoned by the bark, the waitress appeared from somewhere in the back and pulled a pen from behind her ear. She had a lazy eye and graying hair around her forehead. Her apron was stained with something dark red. "Shoot," she said,

225

poised to write down Calman's order. He remembered the time Rizzy had asked him to "shoot." He hoped she was okay.

There were too many choices. Should he be thinking about vitamin content since he didn't have his vitamins with him? He didn't want to. "Um," he said, because the waitress was waiting, looking at him with her lazy eye. "I just want some eggs."

"Scrambled, over-easy, poached, fried? You need to be specific in life, honey. Specific and bold. Check your 'ums' at the door."

Mrs. Blenke chuckled. "Better tell the lady what you want."

"Scrambled," said Calman. He thought he better not ask about egg whites. His mother always ordered egg white omelets and so he did, too, not knowing why he couldn't have yellow ones.

"You got it." The waitress started to walk away when Calman called out, "Chocolate milk!" He looked at Mrs. Blenke, who nodded her approval. "I'd like some chocolate milk, too."

"Brown cow for the cowboy," said the waitress.

Calman couldn't remember the last time he had had chocolate milk, but he liked it a lot and that was the only thing that came to mind when he was coaxed into boldness.

"Should we get you some ice for your head, there?" asked Mrs. Blenke.

"I'm okay."

"Well, then stop touching it. It's not going anywhere."

Calman's bruise was part bump, part scrape, and though it was even more painful when he put pressure on it with his fingers, there was something reassuring and interesting and new about such a texture on his own forehead, not to mention that the sharp pains of life, he was learning, had their advantages over the dull aches.

Simon swung open the diner door and joined them at the table.

"Where's Rizzy?" asked Mrs. Blenke.

"I left her out there."

"You left her?" exclaimed Calman, dropping the spoon he was playing with.

"Now, hold on, son. She's just fine." He sat down next to Eleanor. "I caught a glimpse of her peeking out at me from behind a tree. She'll be back in time." He took a sip of Eleanor's coffee. "This is cold. Where's the waitress?"

"Well, you're awfully calm," said Mrs. Blenke. "How do you know she's okay?"

"She's done this before. You could say it's her signature. She just needs to be alone to think, is all."

"What has she done many times?"

"This big show of getting hurt or running away, but she always comes back. She never really ran away seriously, I think." The waitress came over and poured Simon a cup of coffee. "Thank you, darlin'." He tipped the cup up and into his beard.

So she was faking it? It was possible. After all, it was sudden, it happened right when he said he wanted to go home, and Rizzy had had such an overdose of truths that morning that it was starting to seem out of character for her. He felt duped.

227

"But, really," said Mrs. Blenke, "that doesn't sound right, a girl running away that much. Oscar never had the perfect childhood, if you know what I mean, but he never ran away that I can remember. Why does she run away, Simon?"

"I don't know, Rizzy's complicated," Simon said pensively. "If I had to guess, I'd say it's her mother that's got her wound fiercer than a tornado. Speaking of which, I just called her. She's on her way."

"Here?" said Calman. "Aren't we far away?"

"About four hours or so. She'll likely be here by noon to take you kids home."

"I'll miss my flight," said Calman, thinking out loud.

"They'll put you on another one, not to worry," said Simon.

"It's tough being a parent, if you know what I mean," continued Mrs. Blenke. "Kids can be so unforgiving. I used to say, 'I'm just human,' and Oscar would scream back, 'You're my mother!' I never really knew what to make of that." She looked out the window to some distant place.

"Well, yeah, there's that. I'm sure I wasn't the best father to Lily that I could have been. And living most of her life without a mother. I don't know."

Calman thought of Rizzy on her bike at the penitentiary, her tension, their kiss, her mother, her Level Ten anger, her absence. And he thought of his own mother and her tension, her anger, her absence. He missed them both.

The waitress delivered Calman's plate of eggs and a tall glass of chocolate milk. He ate, clicking silverware to plate, while they all thought.

"But you know," said Mrs. Blenke after a time, "that doesn't explain why you ran away, too." She looked at Calman.

Calman wiped off his chocolate milk mustache with the back of his hand. "Well, we didn't know we were running away. I mean, we just hid out in the car and didn't know you were going to drive away."

"And why were you hiding in the car?" asked Simon.

Calman looked down at his lap and contemplated how he should answer this question. It was easier to place the blame on Rizzy, but the truth was, he had thought about Tank a lot since he saw him lying dead out in the field. He thought maybe Tank was still there, and maybe he and Rizzy were the only ones who still knew that, and that wasn't right. He needed to tell someone. "Um, I don't really remember everything, but I think we may have killed your friend."

"Come again?" said Simon. "Which friend is that?"

"The big one. The one who talks weird."

"Tank. You're saying you killed Tank?"

Eleanor began to say something, but Simon shushed her. Calman looked up to see Simon wink at her, then they both gave him their full attention.

"Well . . . I don't know. Maybe. I think so." He felt like he was being roasted under their full attention. He slouched down in his seat. He touched his bruise. "We, um, I mean me and

Rizzy . . . We were out in the field and saw him out in the field and he was peeing and we scared him and he fell and then I think he wasn't breathing, maybe he had a heart attack and we didn't know what to do, so we left him there and ran and hid in the car, but it was an accident, we didn't mean to scare him, I mean Rizzy didn't mean . . . I mean we didn't mean to kill him." They weren't saying anything. They were just looking at him. "I'm sorry," he said, to fill the void.

Eleanor looked at Simon, Simon pursed his lips and thought, and looked at Calman.

"What . . . what should we do?" asked Calman to break the silence. He couldn't read the expression on Simon's face. He expected to find shock and fury, but thought instead there was a hint of warmth.

"Son," said Simon, clasping his hands around his coffee mug, "Tank's fine. You got nothing to worry about. But beyond that, I'll let Lily fill you in when she gets here."

Calman let out the breath he was holding. "Thank you," he said.

"Well, thank *you* for telling us," said Simon when he finished his coffee. "That was very brave of you." He stood up. "Now I'm going to go make myself seen again—let my granddaughter know we're here for her when she's ready."

After they bought a paper and read the funnies and played word games and spun quarters and took walks outside in pairs and drank more coffee and chocolate milk while contemplating Rizzy's whereabouts and listened to Simon play the banjo and sing his soft folk tunes which the waitress clapped to and said *very nice* and Calman clapped to also and thought *I love this*, Lily swung open the diner door and exclaimed, "Oh, my Lord!" She looked frightfully haggard, as if she had been driving around in a convertible with the top down in a storm. Her gravity-be-damned hair was as wild as Calman had ever seen, where it wasn't wet from sweat and stuck to her scalp. Without makeup, she looked pale, old, and tired. Her red flannel shirt was wrinkled over a dull, washed-out sundress; her sandals were unbuckled.

"Now, take it easy, Lily. You're here. Sit down and have some coffee." Simon pulled up a chair for her.

Lily didn't want to sit. She took a napkin and patted her neck and forehead. "What did I do to deserve this, I ask you. Chasing you all over North America like a bounty hunter, my Lord in heaven, what a day this is turning out to be." She sighed heavily and then surveyed the diner. "Where's Rizzy?"

"Well, now, she's here, she's here, don't you worry," said Simon.

"Where? You said she was with you."

"And she is, she's just taking some alone time, you know your daughter. Come sit down and . . ."

"*Ahh!*" screamed Calman. He had had his back to the window and had turned nonchalantly to look outside to see

Rizzy's lips pressed up against the glass right by his face, her eyes close to his, her fingers clawing at the glass above her head like a lunatic. "That's not funny!"

"Rizzy!" yelled Lily, then she said, more to herself, "Thank God she's okay."

Simon beckoned Rizzy to come inside, luring her with a nod toward their plates of food. "She's got to be hungry," he said.

Rizzy barreled through the door, swung the chair around to sit in it backward, and ordered a club sandwich from the waitress.

"Where were you?" asked Calman.

"None of your business."

"You're not sick?"

"I got better." She said this without looking at him.

"Well, hello to you, too," said Lily. She slid into the booth next to her father and took a sip of water.

Rizzy looked at Lily. "What's with you? You look like crap."

Lily remained uncharacteristically calm. "Thank you," she said.

Calman thought he saw a hint of surprise in Rizzy's eyes, maybe even a smile.

"What are you doing here?" she said, continuing the dialogue with her mother.

"I came to get you, bring you home."

"Maybe we don't want to go home."

"Maybe Calman *does* want to go home," said Mrs. Blenke, looking at Calman.

Calman rested his head against the window. *Yes*, he thought, *I really do want to go home now.*

As if Rizzy could read his thoughts, she said, "Well, maybe I don't want to go home."

"You're a rotten kid," said Lily.

"Thank you."

"Oh, for God's sake, woman," said Simon. "Say what you mean to say to the poor girl. She deserves to hear it."

Lily said, in a softer voice, "All right, all right. I was worried about you. I'm glad you're okay."

"Right," said Rizzy, but there was something different about the way she answered, the way she ping-ponged her glance between Lily and Simon.

At that moment, Lily sneezed loudly and, as sometimes happens with bodily expulsions, her sneeze induced a very unladylike fart.

Rizzy was the first to start laughing, followed by Calman, and eventually all, including Lily.

"Farts," said Lily, "are a funny thing." And that was even funnier to the group.

When it was time to go, after they had eaten lunch and paid the check and lingered outside the diner waiting for Lily to swing her car around, Rizzy didn't put up a fight about going back with Calman and Lily. Lily had told Calman that she had spoken to his mother, who called back to say she had rescheduled her flight from Florida, as well as his flights from Walla Walla and Seattle, and they would meet the next evening at

Boston's Logan International Airport, so they should get going so he could get back to Walla Walla to pack, and Rizzy had said, "Well, let's get going, then," and that was that. Simon and Eleanor were going to continue north, together, until when, they couldn't say, but they'd keep in touch.

"Son, it was great having you around. You're welcome any time," said Simon after a hearty hug.

Calman felt very emotional. He hated goodbyes. "Thank you," he said, which he really meant as a jam-packed thank-you for being friendly and supportive and lighthearted and for playing the banjo and for being someone Calman would be forever glad he had met. "Thank you," he said again.

"Well, Alvin, you've had quite an adventure, after all, I should say." Eleanor took her turn pressing him to her bosom. "I'm very glad I met you. You're a very sweet boy."

"I'm glad I met you, too," said Calman, more to his shoes, and then almost as an afterthought, "Just so you know, my name is really Calman. C.A.L.M.A.N. Not Alvin."

"Calman. Well, I'm glad you told me. Why didn't you tell me that before?"

"I don't know."

Eleanor smiled and touched his cheek. "Well, you're telling me now. Good for you."

Lily pulled the car up and left it running as she hugged her father and thanked him for calling her. "Okay, let's go," she said.

Calman couldn't hold back any longer. "I don't understand. What about your friend Tank?" he said to Simon.

"Oh, right. Lily," he called out, "you better tell them about Tank."

"Tank," said Lily. "Yes, Tank. Apparently, he was very drunk last night and passed out in the field, hit his head on something, but he's fine. Robert is looking after him, not to worry."

"He was drunk," said Rizzy to Calman, smiling.

"Yeah, drunk," said Calman.

He and Rizzy slept most of the way back to Walla Walla. Once, he half awoke and thought he heard Rizzy talking to her mother in a normal kind of way and he had a sense that that was nice and soothing, but he might have been dreaming that, he wasn't sure. He was exhausted.

They arrived in the evening. Rizzy was quiet, sometimes keeping to herself in her bedroom. Calman heard her rummaging about as he packed, the rustling of papers, the clatter of footsteps and dropped boxes. Once or twice she came to him and asked if he wanted what she had in her hand—an old *National Geographic* magazine with an article about the Wild West, the water bottle from her bike, the Japanese fan he forgot to pack, a handful of marbles. He took whatever she gave him, until she lugged the last item around the corner and placed it beside his suitcase.

"Is that your typewriter?" said Calman.

"No, it's a diamond ring, Sherlock. Yeah, it's my typewriter. I want you to take it."

"Why? Don't you need it?"

"No. Who needs a typewriter anymore? We're in the twenty-first century."

"But what about—"

"Forget it. I'm done with that. I never liked romance novels. Investigative journalism is where it's at. All I need is my pad and pencil, and I'm ready to roll. Think I'd make a good journalist?"

"Yeah." Calman wondered if his mother would let him bring the typewriter into the apartment. "Are you going to tell your mother? I mean, about what you've been writing?"

"Probably not. I'll think of some way to wean her off it."

Calman was sitting on Sal's bed, looking down at Rizzy, who was on the floor, reaching her outstretched arms to her toes. He thought back to the first day he had arrived, when he was lying on her bed after having fainted and looking around at his strange surroundings, at his puzzle of a pen pal. That seemed such a long time ago. He picked up Sal's Nerf ball and tossed it at the wall. "Where's Sal?" he asked.

"I don't know. Somewhere. He has a lot of friends he's always hanging out with. Why?"

"He said he would say goodbye."

"He should be back by tomorrow morning." It was a few moments before she asked her next question. "You going to miss him more than me?"

Calman thought about that. He would definitely miss Sal, for Sal was someone so pleasant as to always be missed, like the warmth of the sun during the winter months. But there was something different about the way he'd miss Rizzy, like something he'd worked hard for and could be proud of, a frightful unknown now known and cherished. And anyway, he knew what the answer should be, because he knew what Rizzy needed to hear, knew that he and Rizzy were alike in this way and could help each other, and that maybe in some cosmic sense that was why Sal was away somewhere with all his many friends and Calman was alone in this room with Rizzy. "No," he said. "I'm going to miss you more."

"You going to write to me still?"

"Yeah. Will you write to me?"

"Let's e-mail. I'll e-mail you. I never much liked this letter stuff."

"I can e-mail. But I might still write letters—is that okay? My parents are always on the computer, so it's easier sometimes just to write. I'll type my letters." He nodded toward the type-writer.

"Yeah? Will you write me a romance?"

"Um, maybe." They both smiled and made small noises that sounded like chuckles.

"Will you miss *me*?" asked Calman, feeling his bravest yet on this trip.

"What do you think?" shot back Rizzy.

"I don't know."

Rizzy, he knew in the end, had come to understand what he knew about needs and growth and finding peace. "Yeah," she said. "I wish you weren't going. Maybe next year I'll come visit you in Boston."

"Sure. Yeah, definitely."

"Oh, wait, I have one more thing for you," she said, darting out of the room. In a minute she was back and threw a white T-shirt at him. He unbunched it and held it up. On the front it read, FEMINIST CHICKS DIG ME.

"Is this for me?"

"For you."

"Thanks. Where'd you get it?"

"I stole it from the dork in that convenience store."

Calman laughed. He felt deep satisfaction that he now owned something stolen, something once owned by a bully, and even more satisfaction that she had called the bully a dork. He put the T-shirt on. It was a little big, but he didn't care. This one he wouldn't have to stain.

The next morning, Calman said his goodbyes. Bob shook Calman's hand and wished him luck; Francesca gave him a hug because her mother said she should; and Tank, from his bed in the Dicksons' guest room, told him to watch out for pickpockets, roll-it-up-a-notch. Tank seemed fine, *well* even, as he wrapped his mouth around an overstuffed roast-beef sandwich and channel-surfed.

Sal did come home in time and helped Calman load his suitcase in the car. "It was nice meeting you," said Sal. "Looks like you and Rizzy got along pretty well in the end, eh?"

Calman smiled. He hoped he could be like Sal when he was sixteen. "Yeah," he said. "It was fun. Thanks for being so nice and all. And sharing your room."

"Not a problem. I had a good time, too. You're all right."

Calman took one last look around, the daintiness in the details of the kitchen and living room, the messy front porch filled with children's toys, the backyard with its picnic table and barbecue and Larry's grave, and out to the vast expanse of the onion field, reaching out to the rest of the world. He wanted to remember the onion field, the way it remained steady and strong in sun and in darkness.

And he wanted to remember the last snapshot view of Rizzy and Lily standing side by side in the airport—Lily with her arm around Rizzy's shoulder, both of them waving and watching as he boarded the plane—and the tingling in his cheek where Rizzy had run up at the last minute and given him a kiss, a soft kiss which could have been the reason why, now that he was safely seated in his window seat with, thankfully, no one next to him, Calman was crying.

"Where'd you get that shirt?" said Bridgette Pulowitz, almost immediately after she had dropped her large carry bags, knelt down with open arms, and enveloped Calman in an embarrassing public display of swaying hugs and smacking kisses. She cried out his name so loudly when he emerged from the baggage-claim area that he contemplated ducking into the men's room, but he had a stronger urge to fall into her embrace. He wondered on the flight to Boston if his arrival would be a repeat of what had happened in Walla Walla, that he'd get off the plane and no one would be there to meet him, and this time Mrs. Blenke wouldn't be there either. But his mother was there. How extraordinary it made him feel to discover his mother was there for him. She had arranged it so that her flight from Florida arrived an hour before his flight so they could catch a cab together. Calman's father had taken their original flight the day before so Calman and his mother could be alone.

"Mom, you're tan."

"I was in Florida, honey. Do you like my shirt? I got you one just like it so we can be twins." Passersby took notice of her tall frame, her jet black hair, her attire of bold-colored flowers and dangling shell accessories. Her sunglasses were still atop her head. "So, how are you, favorite son of mine? Tell me everything. Let me look at you. You look pale. Are you feeling okay? Who gave you that shirt?"

"Rizzy did."

"I know all about Rizzy. I spoke to her mother yesterday. What's this about you running away? Were you miserable? You never ran away before. Should I worry? Calman, your forehead! You're bleeding!" Calman's mother worked herself into a tizzy looking for a tissue.

Calman touched his forehead and saw a streak of blood on

his fingers. He ducked when his mother tried to dab at it. "I'm fine," he said. "Here, I'll do it." He took the tissue from her and pressed where the scab had opened.

"How does a boy get a scrape like that? What were you doing? Was someone watching you? Did they check for a concussion? See, I send you away . . ."

"Mom, I'm fine. It doesn't hurt. I don't have a concussion. Scrapes happen." He knew that was an odd thing to say because scrapes didn't happen to him, but he enjoyed saying it.

"Okay, let's deal with this later. Calman, sweetie pie, hurry up and go to the bathroom and rinse your face. Then let's find the taxi stand."

Calman returned from the men's room thinking of his dad. "Mom," he said, "do you have your phone? I want to call Dad."

"Of course, pumpkin, of course." An announcement barked through the cavernous interior of the airport, which was abuzz with voices, rolling luggage, beeps and rings and heels on the hard floor. She handed Calman her cell phone.

"Dad," he said loudly to overcome the noise.

"Calman? Where are you? It's very loud."

"I'm at the airport with Mom." He looked up at his mother standing right by him, watching him. He squatted and spoke facing the floor to gain some privacy.

"Dad, tomorrow's Sunday. Let's do stuff together, can we? Let's go for ice cream or something and hang out." He didn't hear a response so he said, "Dad? Are you still there?"

"I'm still here, son," his dad said quietly, affectionately.

Calman stood back up. "Dad, I can't hear you."

"I said, I'm still here, son, and I would love to spend time with you. I really would. I was thinking the very same thing after you called me last time. We need to do more together, you and me, man to man."

Man to man, thought Calman. It had a nice sound to it. Calman said his goodbyes and handed the phone to his mom. *Yes, he's fine,* he heard her say into the phone. *There's a scrape on his forehead he hasn't explained to me yet, but aside from that he seems—* and here she stopped and really looked at him—*our son seems very grownup.* Calman put his knapsack on and tightened the strap. *I will . . . Yes . . . Yes, I'll remember . . . Okay.* She paused, looking away from Calman, and spoke softly. *Me, too . . . I know . . . we'll see you soon.* "Come on, love," she said to Calman, "let's get a taxi."

His mother talked much like Mrs. Blenke talked on the flight, to fill the time. His mother told him details about her trip, about his grandmother and how they were due for a visit, about the neighbors taking care of the plants in the apartment while they were away. He was listening to the rhythm of her speech.

"Calman," she said, interrupting her own monologue. She was looking at him strangely. "Calman, what are you doing?"

"What do you mean, what am I doing?"

"You're humming, Calman. I can hear you."

"Mom," he said, taking advantage of the break in her chatter, "are you and Dad going to stay married?" His stomach tightened immediately after he asked the question.

She was caught off guard. "Oh, sweetheart, of course." From her bag she took a bottle of lavender oil and rubbed drops onto her temples and between her eyes. She saw Calman was watching her, waiting for a more elaborate answer. "You're a very smart young man," she said, "you know that?" She took a deep breath. "I know we need to sit down and talk about this with you at some point, sugar, but for now . . . Well, listen. The truth is, your father and I have been having problems, that's no secret. But we're not giving up. We do love each other in many ways and we're going to work it out, honey."

He saw tears forming in her eyes and felt such love for her at that moment. "Mom, you and Dad can use what's left of my therapy fund. I don't really want to use it anymore."

Bridgette smiled and reached out to hold his hand. "You know what I think? I think you and I could talk more, what do you think? We could talk more to each other, you and me. About anything, everything, whatever you want to talk about."

"And listen, too," said Calman.

A tear dropped down her cheek. "And listen," she said.

Calman squeezed her hand, then took off his glasses and wiped them clean with his new T-shirt. He looked out the window and saw it was close to sundown. He remembered the sensation of being completely alone out in the night, in a western field. He had been surprised to feel calm instead of panicked, energized instead of paralyzed. He knew he could conjure up that sensation when he needed it. He felt his mother's vulnerability mixed with his own, floating above them as they headed for home. He wasn't afraid. "We'll be okay, Mom," he said.